Emily was a teenager living in Stowe during the 1850s. She fell in love with a young man who, for whatever reason, failed to pass muster with her parents. So the headstrong couple decided to elope, agreeing to meet on the covered bridge at midnight.

Alas, poor Emily soon learned her parents had been right all along. The young man never showed. Too humiliated to go home and too timid to run away alone, the dejected teenager hanged herself from a rafter. Since then her troubled spirit has lingered on the bridge, waiting, getting angrier, weirder, and scarier as the years slip away.

ᴥ Also by Joseph A. Citro ᴖ

ᴥ Fiction ᴖ

Shadow Child*
Guardian Angels
Lake Monsters*
The Gore*
Deus-X: The Reality Conspiracy*
Not Yet Dead*

ᴥ Books That Might Not Be Fiction ᴖ

Green Mountain Ghosts, Ghouls, and Unsolved Mysteries
Passing Strange—True Tales of New England Hauntings and Horrors
Green Mountains, Dark Tales
Cursed in New England: Stories of Damned Yankees
Curious New England: The Unconventional Traveler's Guide to Eccentric Destinations
Weird New England
The Vermont Ghost Guide
The Vermont Monster Guide
Joe Citro's Weird Vermont—Strange Tales of Vermont and Vermonters
Vermont's Haunts—Tall Tales and True from the Green Mountain State

(*indicates titles available from Crossroad Press)

Vermont's Haunts

❧ ❧

**Tall Tales & True
from the Green Mountain State**

Joseph A. Citro

Crossroad Press

❧ CONTENTS ❧

～ SECTION I. ～
THE JOURNEY BEGINS

That venerable Albany, New York anomalist, Charles Fort, has told us, "One measures a circle, beginning anywhere." Okay, but that still leaves the problem of where to begin.

This is a book about Vermont weirdness, so how do we measure that? Do we begin with monsters, madmen, ghosts, curses, strange lands, or eerie legends?

As is so often the case in the realm of the strange, there is no answer. So we'll begin our journey with indecision and we'll dive right into the middle of Mr. Fort's circle.

Hold on!

ᴥ THE SUICIDE GLASS: AN INTRODUCTION ᴦ

As readers of my other books may know, since 1992 I have been systematically collecting Vermont's strangest stories.

In those years—on the radio, on TV, and in a series of books—I have recorded ghost lore, monster tales, historical oddities, and profiles of colorful eccentrics, including murderers, madmen, and miracle workers.

When I speak in public, one question predictably and invariably comes up. Someone will ask, "Has anything weird ever happened to *you*?"

In the past I have tiptoed around that one, suspecting avoidance would enhance my personal air of mystery without compromising my public position of sympathetic skepticism. In retrospect, I should have always answered *yes*, weird things do happen to me. But I have been slow to reveal them in print.

To be precise, exactly four weird things have happened to me in the more than a half-century I've spent on this planet. One during college, the details of which are now lost to a failing memory (though one suspects they are ultimately attributable to a more material kind of "spirit").

The second, from childhood, is most definitely confabulation. I thought I saw a little man peering in the window at me.

The third occurred in bed, a hallucination while in a hypnopompic state. I was dreaming and awake at the same time. This altered condition explains a fair number of similar bedside

3

visitations in the vast ghostlore of our world.

But the fourth and most recent. . . that one remains a mystery.

❧ FESSING UP ❧

I have hesitated to tell this tale for many reasons. For one thing, it is anticlimactic, not nearly as dramatic as a ghost, Bigfoot, or alien encounter. And as a professional storyteller, I hate to disappoint with a second-rate yarn. Also, I hesitate to admit that I didn't behave rationally after it happened. I still cannot explain nor justify my post-weirdness behavior. But I'll get back to that.

And last, I experienced the fear commonly described by many anomaly percipients: the fear that no one will believe me or that I might appear, if not insane, then at least a little less credible.

But enough of the preface; let me tell you what happened. Perhaps someone reading this can offer a rational (i.e. scientific) explanation. I've tried on a few, yet nothing seems to fit.

Stupidly, I did not record the date of the occurrence. It happened about one year after I bought my house in 1993. It must have been in the fall. The windows were closed but as I recall there was no snow on the ground. My best guess is September 1994.

I was alone in the house when the episode began with a muted screech, a constant unwavering sound.

I put down my book and walked over to a southern window that looks out on the driveway, the house next door, and St. Paul Street in Burlington. I thought maybe a siren or car alarm was going off. But as I got closer to the window I realized the noise was coming from inside my house. A smoke alarm, perhaps?

No, because the sound seemed to originate where there was no such alarm. It was in the next room. The kitchen.

As I crossed the threshold, the whine got louder. The sound was elusive. Even in my tiny kitchen I still could not pinpoint exactly where it originated.

I looked at the top of the refrigerator, then down at the kitchen counter. Maybe a timer was going off.

No. That wasn't right, but I did see. . . something.

∽ ∾

Despite the fact that I have a dishwasher, my kitchen counter is typically littered with dirty dishes, cups, and glasses. Everything was in precarious Tower of Pisa piles.

Everything, that is, but the culprit.

At this point I had no doubt what I was hearing, but I had to look two or three times to believe what I was seeing.

One single glass, a thick, squat French tumbler, was spinning on its base. Spinning perfectly, like a top. Slightly angled, though not rocking nor wobbling. Spinning with an aerodynamic certainty so unbelievably fast that it, by itself, seemed to be generating the high-pitched whirring whistle.

I stared at it, nearly hypnotized. I had to stop myself from reaching out to grab it, though it seemed in no danger of falling off the countertop. Although tilted at a slight angel, it remained stolidly in one place.

Then, as I stared, the weirdest thing of all happened: the glass exploded.

It was as if the spinning were caused by an irresistible sympathetic vibration, like a wine glass shattered by an opera singer in a TV commercial.

Was it real or was it Memorex?

It was real. It popped. Shards of glass flew everywhere. I continued to discover them for days: on the floor, behind canisters, under the refrigerator.

But they were not long slivery spikes, as one might expect. They were little cubes, like tiny squares of rock candy. Only the glass's bottom remained, like a jagged monocle, alone, motionless, on the countertop,

And that's the whole story.

∾ A SUICIDAL TUMBLER ∽

I have never been able to identify a reason for the glass to spin so perfectly and so fast. Nor can I discover why such odd behavior in a glass, once started, should result in its exploding.

Unlike the case of the opera singer and the wine goblet, I could pinpoint no source for the sympathetic vibration. My radio, TV, and stereo were off. So was the dishwasher. Although the doomed vessel was on top of it, I can't imagine how the vibration of a non-running dishwasher could set the glass to spinning.

The fact is, the glass seemed to be emitting its own sound, apparently as a result of the spinning. Could it have spun so fast it exploded? If so, it is the only glass in my experience to commit suicide.

What triggered its motion is as big a mystery as why it exploded.

❧ DR. DON ❧

I discussed the whole incident with my neighbor, a scientist at SUNY Plattsburgh. Luckily he knows me well enough to take such an outlandish story seriously. Dr. Donald Slish said, "My first thought was that maybe you had a vivid dream and confused it with reality. But you kept finding glass—dreams don't leave evidence."

I agreed. But, but the question remained: "What could have caused it?"

Don shook his head. "I would probably guess that it was some kind of weird physical phenomenon that is so rare that it hasn't been, and could never be, studied. We know an awful lot about the common things but it's possible that there are many rare things that we know nothing about. The real question is how can such things be studied when they occur rarely and non-repeatably?"

He had eloquently summed up the essence of my life's work.

❧ POST-WEIRDNESS BEHAVIOR ❧

None of our mysteries will ever be understood if they are studied by "scientists" like me. I have been researching the unknown for at least fifteen years and yet, when I had my own experience, I made all the mistakes that I have criticized others for making. I did not record the precise date and time of the occurrence. I failed to make timely descriptive notes, ignoring the atmosphere and environment. I didn't even have the good sense to gather up the broken glass and save it as evidence.

Somehow, at the time, the whole thing seemed oddly normal, akin to dropping and breaking some inexpensive tumbler. It wasn't until some time afterward that I thought, *What the hell just happened?*

In the entire scheme of world weirdness, I can only conclude by questioning the unremarkable nature of this seemingly insignificant event. Bigfoot sightings, UFO reports, and ghost stories are weird, but are they any weirder than a singing, exploding tumbler?

Keep reading and judge for yourself. . .

❧ DON'T OPEN THE WINDOW! ❧

*"I look in at the windows of
Heaven and see all that there
is in the invisible world."*
—Mother Ann Lee, founder of the Shakers

For years investigators of strange phenomena have theorized that certain places, like certain people, can be extraordinarily vulnerable to "mysterious forces."

Diverse labels have been used to describe these "haunted" areas. My favorite, of course, would be "Twilight Zones." But long before Rod Serling, that eldritch New England horror master, H.P. Lovecraft, discussed "dimensional gateways."

Among Fortean researchers we note the terrifying speculations of John A. Keel, who used the term "Windows" or "Window Areas" to describe the presumed interdimensional trapdoors. Zoologist Ivan Sanderson one-upped Mr. Keel when he coined the slightly more sinister "Vile Vortices."

Ever since Vincent Caddis's term "Bermuda Triangle" became part of our language, writers have co-opted "Triangle" to designate any odd geographical area.

Maine researcher Loren Coleman identified Massachusetts's "Bridgewater Triangle." I even swiped the term when I wrote about Vermont's own "Bennington Triangle."

Twilight Zones. Vile Vortices. Unholy Triangles. Of these terms, it seems to me, the most useful is also the most benign: "Window Areas." These are places where a porthole seems to be open between this world and some other.

Chancing a glance into one of these windows, a human being might see any assortment of anomalies, from angels to pterodactyls to flying saucers. Or, one might perceive more earth-bound enigmas like lake monsters, glowing virgins, or shambling eight-foot man-beasts. The more out of sync the apparitions are with our conventional three dimensional reality, the more conspicuous they become.

Vermont, like every New England state, has its share of Window Areas. I have identified at least three, and several more that are "suspect."

The first, and perhaps largest, might be the glassy waters of Lake Champlain. The land around the hundred-plus-mile lake may well be the frame around a window to another world.

The most mainstream of Lake Champlain's many anomalies is of course the infamous Lake Champlain Monster, or monsters, popularly known as "Champ" (or "Champs"). For hundreds of years these uncatchable serpents have been dodging nets while generating tales. The evidence seems overwhelming, but doubt lingers. And proof remains nonexistent. Whatever swims in the lake's cold dark waters remains one of Vermont's most enduring mysteries.

The sky above the lake also generates a puzzling variety of sightings. Giant birds with oddly reptilian features have been spotted over northern waters.

UFOs are frequently seen actually entering or leaving the lake. Students of such things speculate there's a UFO base somewhere underwater. Well, maybe. . .

A fair number of "abductions" have been reported on Champlain. For example, in 1968 two teenagers were snatched from a dock belonging to Buff Ledge, a private girl's camp north of Burlington. They reappeared with escalating agitation and holes in their memories.

In 1978 scientist Walter Webb of Boston's Hayden Planetarium began a five year study of the case. He even published a book about the incident: Encounter at Buff Ledge (1994). Although all the details checked out, I'm not certain whether the definitive solution to this and similar mysteries will come from a physicist, a psychiatrist, a folklorist, or a theologian.

≪ ≫

The second Vermont "Window Area" is what I have termed "The Bennington Triangle." Though not literally triangular, this vast stretch of undeveloped land includes the mysterious Glastenbury Mountain, an area long considered "troubled." It's plagued by weird shapes, horrible sounds, unidentifiable odors, unrecognizable animals, ghostly apparitions, and dramatic monster sightings.

After a series of inexplicable vanishings in the late 1940s and early 1950s, news of this disturbed and disturbing land reached statewide, even national, media. There were at least six disappearances in all. More, according to some counts. And when these individuals vanished, they were gone so thoroughly it was as if they had stepped off the edge of the earth. Thousands of determined searchers found not a trace.

Everyone was puzzled, not to mention edgy. As *The Bennington Banner* wrote following the disappearance of Freida Langer: "One of the things hard to explain is how Mrs. Langer could have become so completely lost in an hour's time before dark in an area with which she was so thoroughly familiar."

A half-dozen or more people, gone, as if they'd blinked out of existence. How can we possibly explain it? Well, we might say, they were in a window area. Did something reach out and pull them through?

Vermont's third "Window Area" is a stretch of land around Gold Brook in Stowe—the area of Stowe Hollow Bridge. This scenic covered bridge, known far and wide as "Emily's Bridge," has for years been a magnet for weird tales.

An array of odd events has taken place there, including sounds with no source, words uttered from nowhere, cold drafts on hot days, hats and personal belongings whisked away or vanishing, lights dancing about in an inexplicable manner, spontaneous equipment failure, deliberate wounds to animals and people. And perhaps most dramatic of all, spirit materializations. Sometimes these images are even recorded in photographs or on video

All these odd acts are attributed to the ghost of Emily. As one story goes, the poor girl—always without a last name—was jilted on that bridge around 1850. Supposedly her lover failed to appear for their midnight rendezvous. Perhaps overreacting a bit, Emily hanged herself from a rafter and has been appearing at unpredictable intervals ever since, getting angrier and angrier as the decades flit past.

My theory is that Emily is a fiction.

There are just too many conflicting stories to explain her death. Some maintain Emily was murdered there. Others say she jumped from the bridge in a seizure of suicidal depression. Another scenario involves her being thrown from her horse and dying slowly on the rocks below. Her cries, they say, can be heard to this day.

Since no one, historian, scientist, nor psychic, has ever been able to produce any evidence that "Emily" ever existed, or died, I have concluded that the story of Emily's ghost is a contrivance, developed incrementally over the years and retrofit to explain all the mysterious happenings that, otherwise, would have occurred without rationale in and around the bridge.

So I would call Emily's Bridge and environs a "Window Area" rather than a haunted spot. By removing Emily from the equation we still have myriad mysteries occurring there.

And, according to a growing collection of files, Emily's Bridge continues to provoke more odd incidents than any other spot in Vermont.

⁀ SEARCHING FOR EMILY ⁀

I keep the notion of "Window Areas" pretty much to myself because in today's popular culture "hauntings" are far more sexy and fun. But whenever I am asked to name the most haunted, disturbed, or troubled spot in Vermont, I quickly nominate that certain covered bridge in Stowe. Its formal name is the Gold Brook Bridge. Some call it the Stowe Hollow Bridge. But for most people it will always be Emily's Bridge, because, as we have seen, Emily is the ghost who supposedly haunts it.

The bridge's "Most Haunted" status is based on the sheer number of ghostly anecdotes generated by this one particular location. And, because of the nature of those reports, Emily's Bridge is perhaps the most consistently puzzling of Vermont's many "haunted" sites.

On the off chance that someone reading this has not heard the story, or if you skipped the previous chapter, here is a brief summary:

Emily was a teenager living in Stowe during the 1850s. She fell in love with a young man who, for whatever reason, failed to pass muster with her parents. So the headstrong couple decided to elope, agreeing to meet on the covered bridge at midnight.

Alas, poor Emily soon learned her parents had been right all along. The young man never showed. Too humiliated to go home and too timid to run away alone, the dejected teenager hanged herself from a rafter. Since then (so the story goes) her troubled spirit has lingered on the bridge, waiting, getting angrier, weirder, and scarier as the years slip away.

There are variations of the story, of course. Some say Emily was murdered there. Some describe here suicide as a fatal jump from the bridge. Another scenario blames the whole thing on an accident: either she's thrown from a horse or she topples her wagon, tumbles over the rocks, and dies slowly in the river. Her eerie pleas for help, some say, echo ruefully across the centuries.

Scores of people claim they've had run-ins with Emily. But so far no one—even the most dedicated of researchers—has been able to *prove* that Emily actually lived. Or died. The bridge is there, all right, but Emily is not a historical fact.

One Stowe woman even claims to be Emily's mother. That is, she says she gave birth to the story around 1970 when she concocted it to scare a bunch of students from the nearby college, Johnson State.

Though many evidential anecdotes take place in horse-and-buggy days, it seems odd that the oldest printed account I've been able to find is from a now-deceased weekly newspaper dated 1983. However, my research shows that the bridge was thought to be haunted at least as far back as 1948.

I suspect the Stowe woman may have named the ghost, but it's unlikely she created it.

So the *truth* of all this may be a little fuzzy, but the fact is that Emily's Bridge continues to provoke more odd incidents than any other spot in Vermont.

A whole spectrum of supernatural events has been reported there, ranging from the benign to the malevolent. For example, harmless lights from nowhere flitter around the bridge's interior. Disembodied voices speak. Hats detach from heads and soar away. Cold spots manifest on warm summer days.

More menacing are the spontaneous wounds said to afflict livestock, and sometimes people, crossing the bridge at night.

I have seen dozens of photographs showing mysterious streaks, floating orbs, and wispy female-like forms.

Recently an out-of-state tourist showed me a picture he'd

taken of the bridge. He'd heard none of the ghost stories; he just wanted to photograph the bridge because it's pretty. Imagine his bewilderment when his finished photo included the image of a girl who, he swears, was not there when he snapped the shutter.

Many times I have personally ventured to Stowe Hollow in hopes of a face-to-face confrontation with the supernatural. Because I have never happened to run into Emily, I must conclude, sadly, that I'm not the young man she's waiting for. But a mysterious incident in the spring of 2000 made me think my luck might be changing. I got a phone call from a man who'd come directly from Emily's bridge. "I could hear music there," he told me excitedly. "Faraway music. It was the weirdest thing...!"

Eager to hear this "celestial symphony" for myself, I jumped into my car and made the one-hour drive from Burlington to Stowe. Maybe this time I'd meet Emily

After parking near the bridge I looked around, listening carefully for any possible source of strange music. Everything was silent. Natural sounds prevailed. There was no evidence of far-off radio, stereo, or TV sound.

But the moment I stepped across the threshold and onto the wooden planks of the bridge I could indeed hear... something. It sounded like a faraway tinkling, vaguely Asian, almost like a distant wind chime.

For the life of me I couldn't determine the source of those gentle musical tones.

Weirder still, as I moved around the bridge I discovered spots where I could hear the music and other spots where I *could not*. There was no denying it: ethereal music was really in the air.

If I had about-faced and headed for home right then I would have had a brand new ghost story about Emily's Bridge. Instead, I held my ground, determined to find a natural cause... if one was available.

After I had explored every inch of the bridge's interior I decided to check underneath. In a moment the solution was obvious, not to mention anticlimactic.

It is a bridge, after all. Water runs underneath. I soon discovered a nearly vertical concave rock against which water was occasionally splashing. When splashed with sufficient force, the concavity reflected some of the water back into a standing pool, causing the faint musical tinkling. The weird acoustics of the bridge did the rest.

The musical phenomenon wasn't constant. It only happened when a rush of water hit the rock just so. At another time of year, when the water level was higher, or lower, it might not have happened at all.

But on this windless spring day Gold Brook was flowing just right. And the music of the spheres could be heard on Emily's Bridge.

Upon reflection, one wonders how many of the other ghostly phenomena reported on this bridge are the result of overreaction, misperception, or inadequate investigation. Who can say?

All we know for sure is that if Emily's Bridge is not the most haunted spot in Vermont, it is certainly more famous than all its contenders. Emily's story has spread far and wide through books, TV, radio shows.

For some reason, poor Emily just can't get across that bridge. And we can't seem to get over it.

⇜ IRA ALLEN, GHOSTBUSTER ⇝

Anyone interested in the sort of "outsider information" presented in this and my other books has probably noticed the recent proliferation of so-called "Paranormal Groups" and "Paranormal Investigators." It's a worldwide phenomenon that can be traced to a TV show, *Ghost Hunters*, that premiered in 2004. (I think it can be traced farther back, to 19th century Spiritualism, séances, and psychic investigators, but that's another story.)

We have at least three such groups of specter detectors here in Vermont. So I got to wondering who Vermont's first ghost hunter might have been. So far the outstanding candidate is Ira Allen, brother of Ethan, "Father of the University of Vermont," and one of the founders of the state.

In his autobiography Ira talks about some friends he met in the early 1770s, a mother with two lovely daughters. He writes, "[They] used to amuse me by telling... frightful stories [of ghosts and apparitions...] amongst which were many stories [about] an old woman... without a head.

Now here's where the ghost hunting comes in. Ira writes, "One evening I challenged the old woman without a head, and all the ghosts, to meet me at any time and place they chose."

This bravado alarmed Ira's friends. The young women warned him not to provoke the spirits or there would be supernatural retaliation. And soon.

The very next day some of Ira's hogs escaped. As darkness fell, he went to round them up, following their tracks along a snowy footpath leading deep into the forest.

As it got later he trudged deeper into the darkening woodland; he estimated about three miles. His progress was slowed by about four inches of snow on the ground.

Ira admits that thoughts of the headless woman crossed his mind. What would he do if he saw her? Would he run? Hold his ground? Step forward and challenge her?

Well, he was about to find out. There she was, right in front of him.

He says, "to my no small surprise, at about eight rods distance, I...[saw] the perfect appearance of a woman without a head; her shoulders, waist, arms akimbo, her hands on her hips, woman's clothes, and feet below were in perfect shape...; all which I viewed with astonishment."

Could it be real? "If the God of nature authorizes apparitions," Ira wrote, "then there is no flying from them."

With that he raised his cane and advanced, prepared to deliver a punishing blow.

He says, "I came within about 30 yards before I discovered the cause..."

He found that a tree had been broken off by the wind, leaving a human-sized stump. Some of its bark had fallen away, creating the illusion of a white dress. Above that, a dappled pattern—the work of woodcocks—completed the upper torso. The night made the darker areas invisible, forming, Ira wrote, "the size and figure of a headless woman."

To satisfy himself, he turned around and went back to the original spot. From there the headless woman was visible again.

And then Ira Allen writes a line that perhaps reveals the source of a lot of ghost stories. He wrote, "Had I been frightened and run away, I might, like others, have believed in spectral appearances."

So there you have it: Vermont's first ghost, busted.

⁓ EDDYS: FROM THE OTHER SIDE ⁓

*A new look at the Eddy Brothers' séances
from a skeptical perspective. Featuring
more classic Vermont Ghostbusters...*

No one driving through Chittenden, Vermont would ever suspect it's a town with a dark secret. At the mystery's epicenter, an unremarkable two-story wood-frame building. Over the years it has been a tavern, a farm, a private home, and an inn. Its most recent incarnation is as a ski club, refurbished now and modestly elegant. But a century and a quarter ago—during the glory years of American Spiritualism—locals shunned the place, calling it the home of the devil.

Within its dingy walls two sullen, nearly illiterate brothers, William and Horatio Eddy, along with their sister Mary, conducted an amazing series of séances that baffled investigators while attracting spiritualists and skeptics from around the world.

Today the brothers are nearly forgotten. Most Chittenden residents don't know the story; others refuse to discuss it. Though they are routinely ignored in Spiritualist histories, the Eddy brothers were never effectively debunked. And plenty of people tried.

⁓ COLONEL OLCOTT ⁓

The most influential investigator was Col. Henry Steel Olcott. In 1874, this inquisitive New York attorney visited the brothers and described his experiences in the *New York Sun*. Another paper, the *New York Daily Graphic*, sensed the story's commercial potential. They sent Col. Olcott back to Chittenden for ten weeks to determine whether the Eddys were villains or visionaries. His fascinating twice-a-week articles quickly tripled the paper's circulation.

Henry Steel Olcott was something of a Renaissance man, an intellectual hybrid of scientist, soldier, lawyer, playwright, journalist, and scholar. Above all, and most important: he was an accomplished detective.

The phenomena he witnessed at the Eddy farmhouse were so complicated and diverse that it is difficult to give a succinct accounting. Col. Olcott said he observed every manifestation known to psychic science including spirit rappings and writing, prophesy, human levitation, teleportation, remote vision, and more. But most amazing and controversial were the full-body materializations. Every night of the week, except Sunday, spirits walked the floors of the Eddy farmhouse.

A typical séance began when William finished washing the supper dishes. Guests and visitors assembled in the 17 by 35 foot "circle room" above the kitchen. Up to 100 spectators seated on wooden benches faced a platform lighted by a dim kerosene lamp.

William would mount the platform and state, "I am ready." He'd enter the tiny closet he called his "spirit cabinet." For a suspenseful moment everyone waited, silent with anticipation. Soon soft voices spoke or sang in the distance. Shortly, from behind the curtained door of William's cabinet, ethereal forms began to emerge at roughly five minute intervals. Twenty, even thirty in the course of an evening. Some were completely visible and seemingly solid. Others only partially materialized. Still others remained transparent as they paraded before the open-mouthed spectators.

The apparitions varied in size from that of an infant, to well over six feet (William was only 5'9"). Certain ghostly visitors— elderly Vermonters and American Indians—appeared night after night like members of a spectral repertory troupe. But others appeared as well—black Africans, Russians, Kurds, Asians and more—all in native dress, many speaking their native tongue.

Then, in a wild vaudevillian carnival of souls, the apparitions performed: singing, dancing, chatting with the spectators; they'd magically produce weapons, scarves, and musical instruments. Some even told jokes. One "spirit conundrum" began when a sepulchral voice asked, "Can you tell me why the devil cannot skate?"

A spectator replied, "I'm sorry, I cannot."

The spirit's punch line: "How in hell can he?"

But ghostly burlesque productions were not why the spectators came; they wanted to see relatives and friends who had "passed over." And they were rarely disappointed; reunions took place night after night. Loved ones long gone emerged from the tiny cabinet. They waved, spoke, and occasionally embraced their living visitors.

Col. Olcott was stumped. Where did the apparitions come from? If they were William in various disguises, how could he so dramatically alter his height and form? If they were William's accomplices, how did they slip unseen into the sealed cabinet?

He rigorously examined William's cramped closet, but found only plaster and lathe. No trapdoors, no hidden compartments, no room for anyone but the medium himself.

In all, Col. Olcott witnessed over 400 materializations. He judged such a show, night after night, would require a whole company of actors and several trunks full of costumes. Yet repeated inspections—often with the aid of hired carpenters and engineers—disclosed no place to hide people or props.

Additionally, such elaborate shows would be expensive. The Eddy's would have to pay actors, purchase costumes, and buy expensive "magical illusions." Yet they appeared poor, did all the housework themselves, and charged only eight dollars a week for room and board. Many people were accommodated for free. No one ever paid for the séances.

Though Col. Olcott came to Chittenden a skeptic, he left a believer. He grew to dislike the gloomy brothers, but he was absolutely convinced of their mysterious power. The next year, 1875, he documented his conversion experience in a 500-page book called *People from the Other World.*

Most of what we know about the Eddys comes from that book.

Col. Olcott did lazy researchers a great favor by consolidating Eddy family history and a detailed overview of their performances in a single volume. His comprehensive compilation of descriptions, testimonials, diagrams and pictures leaves the reader with the clear impression that what happened in Chittenden was on the level—hard, cold, scientific fact. His endorsement turned William and Horatio Eddy into international psychic superstars.

At the same time there was an aggressive contingent of skeptics whose conclusions are often overlooked by those who have told the Eddys' story.

❧ DR. GEORGE M. BEARD ❧

The most ruthless and outspoken critic, Dr. George M. Beard of New York City, was the Amazing Randi of his day. More debunker than investigator, Dr. Beard never entertained the possibility that the materializations might be genuine.

After disguising himself, hoping to appear simple-minded, Dr. Beard visited Chittenden in October of 1874. After watching one séance, he then quickly dismissed the Eddys as inept tricksters.

Dr. Beard argued that because the materializations were conducted in such poor light, they were impossible to see and therefore totally bogus. "I could not have recognized my nearest and dearest friends, eight or ten feet from me."

His conclusion: all the manifestations, from infant to giant, were "personations" by William Eddy.

Never one to mince words, the good doctor concluded that witnesses, "...are so blind, or so stupid, or so prejudiced, that their opinions on the subject are entirely worthless."

❧ A VERMONTER INVESTIGATES ❧

Vermont newspaper editor Lucius Bigelow of *The St. Albans Daily Advertiser*, was not satisfied with Col. Olcott's investigation. He also wanted to test the validity of Dr. Beard's conclusions. As gentleman and loyal Vermonter, Mr. Bigelow felt the reliability of Dr. Beard's "expose" was compromised by "the flippantly unjust picture he drew of the inhabitants of Chittenden."

Determined to see for himself, Mr. Bigelow rounded up a couple of trusted cronies—"men of marked acuteness and high intelligence"—and on November 21, 1874 the trio set out for Chittenden. In his four column exposé, Mr. Bigelow generally agreed with Dr. Beard, dismissing Col. Olcott's account as a fairy tale. Like Dr. Beard, Mr. Bigelow contended that William had "personated" all eighteen manifestations. He also agreed that the light was so dim that identifying the materializations was impossible. However, a young lady from Illinois, several feet farther away, had no trouble recognizing three different relatives in the same light. Editor Bigelow wrote, "...my two friends and myself, sitting on the second bench from the front, could distinguish no features nor even faces, nor note colors with sufficient distinctness to accurately describe dress while the lady in question could see a soldier [her father!] with perfect plainness."

Mr. Bigelow used her and other overly credulous witnesses as grounds to dismiss all the testimony Col. Olcott had collected. He wrote, "[T]he ability of certain infatuates in the audience to distinguish friends is a pitiable exhibition of credulity and excited imagination."

Perhaps more damning, Lucius Bigelow clearly recognized William and Horatio as "the same jugglers [i.e. tricksters] that, with their sister [most likely Mary], gave exhibitions in Burlington, Vermont some nine years ago, and were there detected in their imposition...."

❧ MARY EDDY EXPOSED ❧

Writer Thomas R. Hazard recalled witnessing another exposure of the Eddys while they were on tour during the 1860s. A skeptical doctor on the investigating committee had secretly filled a syringe with ink. During the séance, just as a "spectral arm" extended mysteriously from the spirit cabinet, the doctor let fly a jet of black liquid. He then grabbed Mary Eddy and dragged her toward the spectators, displaying the telltale stains on her wrist.

Mr. Hazard wrote, "I never shall forget the scene that then transpired. There stood the medium seemingly in blank amaze, not only convicted of fraud, but caught in the very act; and there stood the burly doctor elate with his victory.... But the scene soon shifted. Casting her eye on her accuser, the medium ... [seized] her exposer by the nape of the neck, she sent him whirling around the platform as easily as ... Samson (with whose spirit she was perhaps possessed) could fling a cat."

❧ NOW HORATIO ☙

Of course trickery was far more difficult to discover in the controlled environment of the Eddy homestead. Nonetheless there are blatant examples on record. On September 9, 1873 a skeptical Boston Spiritualist visited the farm. Secretly armed with two matches each, he and five accomplices attended one of Horatio's "dark séances."

Horatio was tied securely in a chair next to some musical instruments. When the room was blackened, music began to come from a guitar. The instrument sailed around as it played, seemingly borne by spirit hands. On cue the investigator lit his match to reveal "...Horatio G. Eddy ... with guitar in hand.... He instantly turned and threw the guitar at my head, and, as I expected, put out my match. By this time all the others had lighted, and he was seen retreating by the empty chair crouching down as much as possible so as to deceive the eye as to his form. No sane person can think we may have been mistaken as we had the assisted light of six brilliant parlor matches."

The conspirators left Chittenden, forever convinced the séances were "an unmitigated fraud."

❧ DAMNED AT LAST ❧

The most damaging article was published in *The New York Sun* on November 22, 1875, a year after Bigelow and Beard. The same newspaper that had given birth to the Eddy phenomenon now dealt its deathblow. Titled "Exposure of the Eddys," it was written with such sincerity and conviction that it sounded like the last word on the subject. Reprints quickly appeared in dozens of newspapers all over the country.

The writer agreed with Col. Olcott and Dr. Beard: "The battle regarding the materializations must be fought at the spirit cabinet door." Clearly, the numerous ghostly forms emerging from within had to be: (1.) deceptive impersonations by William Eddy, (2.) actors in disguise, or (3.) manifestations of an occult force. As Col. Olcott stated, "There is no escape from the syllogism."

Wisely, the writer refuted Dr. Beard's thesis by admitting the various spirits could not have been the burly William Eddy in disguise—their forms, frames, and behaviors were simply too diversified. So if the forms were not ghosts and not William, they had to be actors. Until this point no one had been able to demonstrate how accomplices could gain access to the cabinet undetected. Here the debunker broke new ground: "I will...show ... its very simple method of execution." So simple, he gloated, "that it is perfectly astonishing it could ever have stood the observation of one man or woman not blinded by overfaith and childish credulity."

❧ THE BIFURCATED CHIMNEY ❧

William's spirit cabinet was in reality a closet constructed on the elevated platform between a central chimney and the wall. Its dimensions were 2'7" by 7'.

The exposer claimed to have noticed the floorboards within the cabinet were laid in the opposite direction from the boards of the platform on which it stood. Why should that be? The cabinet and the platform shared the same floor.

It was, he said, because the cabinet contained a false floor designed so William could enter, cover the doorway with a blanket, "...and lo! nearly all of the cabinet floor glides noiselessly under the outside platform, being moved by somebody underneath. There is now revealed... an opening in the chimney large enough to admit the passage of a human body. By close, narrow stairs you can descend through the chimney to the kitchen below. The chimney is made in two compartments; one for the materialized spirits to go up and down, and one for the smoke of the kitchen stove to ascend."

It was a neat, logical explanation. It settled the case for skeptics. By the end of 1875 even true believers began to doubt the "sainted" pair.

❧ PROBLEMS WITH THE SOLUTION ❧

But there are a few things about the writer, the article, and the explanation that seem a bit suspicious. First, the "exposer" fails to identify himself. His (or possibly her) "expose" was mailed from Rutland on November 22, but we never learn exactly when he or she visited the Eddy home.

The writer claims to have attended séances in the circle room, however it is never clearly stated that he actually examined the floor and chimney of the spirit cabinet, nor does anyone corroborate his disclosure. He simply says, "A visit to the Eddys recently, at a season when the electrical conditions of the atmosphere were very favorable for the exhibition of spirit power, enabled me to form a clear and definite idea of how the thing was done...."

It sounds more like divine revelation than legitimate investigation, but readers who had tired of the Eddy controversy didn't care that an "idea" is not a proof, or that a "theory" is not a fact. In spite of the writer's slippery diction, the article had the ring of truth and was as devastating as any legitimate exposure of fraud.

However, one fact consistently reported by all the papers is that during the day the Eddys' séance room, platform, and spirit cabinet were continually available for examination. Every visitor to the Eddy home was free to poke and prod to his or her heart's content. Of course, trapdoors and secret panels were the first thing everyone looked for.

In a rebuttal letter to *The New York Sun*, Col. Olcott wrote, "The fact is that not only once but several times, I examined the flooring of the cabinet where I could not only see but actually tested the solidity of every board and joist, and did this once in company with a Massachusetts inventor, who has many patents for mechanical contrivances, and who was not a Spiritualist; and once with a Hartford architect."

What's more, the drawings in Col. Olcott's book clearly show that all the floorboards, inside and outside the cabinet, are in identical alignment.

❧ A HOUSE DIVIDED ❧

By itself the bifurcated chimney theory was not enough to finish off the Eddys. Other factors contributed equally to their fall from grace.

First, on a nationwide basis, phony spirit mediums were being denounced right and left. The press, once enthralled by "psychic revelations," discovered debunkings more entertaining and therefore more lucrative. Public curiosity waned as theatrical spiritualism began its long decline.

The next important factor was foreshadowed in the Mary Eddy exposure mentioned above. Apparently the Eddys were a wild old family. Just as Mary beat-up on the doctor, the Eddys began beating-up each other. The Rutland Herald reported an 1873 Christmas party at the Eddy homestead during which a fight broke out. Webster, the youngest Eddy brother, bested Horatio. William got into the act, sided with Webster, and Horatio received a second drubbing.

By 1876 the family had fallen apart. In a 1980 interview, Agnes Gould, a ninety-six year old Chittenden resident, recalled how the Eddys feuded and eventually split up, "They'd get jealous of each other's power, each other's success."

Sister Mary moved to East Pittsford where she gave séances of her own. William packed up and headed for Colorado. And Horatio stayed on at the farm in Chittenden where he tried to mend his damaged reputation.

In a letter to the *Sun* dated February 15, 1876, Horatio denied the existence of the trapdoor and divided chimney. He invited the editor to come to Chittenden to see for himself, offering $1000.00 if he could find evidence of fraud. Horatio closed by threatening a libel suit.

The editor laughed it off. "Now chimneys are very uncertain creatures. We have known them to undergo startling changes... Although we do not think we are mistaken in Mr. Eddy's character, we are not prepared to trust his chimney...."

Following Horatio's next "indignant and ungrammatical" letter, the Sun wrote, "...we beg to be permitted to continue to regard Mr. Horatio G. Eddy as an impudent humbug."

After that they ignored him completely.

ৎ৶ ৵ঌ

So the question remains, were the Eddys humbugs or heroes?

Common sense demands that we view them as clever fakes, ingenious stage magicians who misapplied their art. Their credibility was thoroughly impeached by a pattern of chicanery. But one fact remains: no one was ever able to successfully explain how William Eddy produced a series of three-dimensional apparitions from a closed, sealed closet.

Col. Olcott was certain its walls and floor were properly solid. Dr. Beard, after his own examination, agreed: "Col. Olcott is right when he says that it is impossible for any one to go into the cabinet from outside."

Further, numerous accounts testify that William was able to do exactly the same thing at other locations—locations he was never given an opportunity to prepare.

And the spirits? Well, in time they stepped out of the shadows and appeared in full light. Honto, the acrobatic "Indian girl," even permitted herself to be photographed.

Unfortunately, most of the written and photographic evidence has been burned, buried, or lost. The house itself was long ago divided, literally converted into two houses. At that time the spirit cabinet, platform and chimney were dismantled, their materials burned or recycled. And the people in Chittenden, those few who are old enough to remember, have forgotten or refuse to talk.

Col. Olcott was never convinced that the Eddy apparitions were actually the spirits of the dead. A careful reading of his book shows he remained open-minded to the end.

Today, his final analysis is as good as it was in 1874. He wrote, "The forms I saw at Chittenden, while apparently defying any other explanation than that they are of super-sensual origin, are still as a scientific fact to be regarded as 'not proven.'"

❧ SECTION II. ❧
GHOSTLY GHETTOES

Wherein we look at some places where ghosts seem to gather. Not individual ghosts. Not haunted houses. But rather Vermont places that might be called ghost towns, specter collectives, spiritual settlements.

They're nearby and all over the state.

And this is by no means a complete census.

❧ DEAD AT DARTMOUTH ❧

They dwell in that disputable land between fact and fancy, reality and imagination, college and the real world. They are the hidden population on every campus: phantoms, wraiths, and revenants of students who simply cannot pick up their diplomas and leave.

❧ HUNTING FOR HAUNTS ❧

The real mystery of Dartmouth's ghosts is why there are so few. Yale has their invisible organist whose unexpected Woolsey Hall recitals routinely baffle faculty and students. Harvard has a veritable troupe of Victorian phantoms lurking around Thayer Hall, and an erudite specter at Massachusetts Hall who holds conversations with students and deans.

So why not Dartmouth? Their admission requirements for spectral scholars must be unusually rigorous: ghosts are nearly impossible to find. My multiple queries to professors, staff, and students invariably yielded similar replies:

"Ghosts? Not at Dartmouth."

"I don't know why, but we don't seem to have them."

"I'm not sure my boss would want me talking about it."

"Please don't use my name . . ."

If there isn't a campus wide gag order then perhaps the college elects to keep its preternatural population well off campus, confining their most menacing example to the slopes of Mount

31

Moosilauke. There the Outing Club annually summons the spirit of Doc Benton and tales of his sinister shenanigans. (See *Passing Strange* by Joseph A. Citro, pgs.220-230.)

But closer to the Green—despite secrecy, censorship, or the best efforts of Safety and Security—the occasional student has a run-in with a ghost. Sketchy stories persist about a presence in Baker Library. Some say the top floor, the one under the bell tower, is the haunted spot. According to a long-held rumor, anyone trespassing there is likely to hear unsettling noises. Stashed somewhere is the alleged proof: audio tapes of these otherworldly sounds.

In April of 2002, an unidentified student told *The Dartmouth* (the oldest college newspaper in America), "I had a very strange experience on the seventh floor... I was looking at one of the shelves, which was full of books. I looked down, and then up again. The shelf was empty."

A more tangible incident occurred in late July, 2002. Two registration workers at the Blunt Alumni Center were preparing for Alumni College. Upon rising, one noticed something odd in the Zimmerman Lounge. "Come over here," she said to her companion. "Take a look at this."

The second woman crossed to the door and looked in. "I just screamed," she told me. "I said, 'Oh my word!'"

There, in a cushioned chair, was the perfect image of a man. His head was most visible. Both women saw his large hat. His expression suggested displeasure.

Later, they tried to figure out who he was and why he appeared so unhappy. After consulting a book about the dormitories, one woman thought she knew.

"What dorm are we not using?" she asked her companion.

"Andres. We're not using Andres."

With that she pointed to a photograph in the book. Sure enough, their vision exactly matched the portrait of F. William Andres (1929), former chair of trustees (circa 1979).

❧ THE TOMB ROOM ❧

Even the uninitiated stop to stare at the columned mansion at 9 School Street. Older alumni may remember it as Phi Sigma Psi, as it was known during much of the 19th and 20th centuries. Today the 1835 edifice houses "Panarchy," one of Dartmouth's two undergraduate societies.

Could it house something more?

Two explanations account for its inexplicable disturbances.

One recalls its days as a private residence. Its owner, a wealthy physician, harbored a dark secret: he kept his crazed daughter locked in the attic. Ill-treatment, loneliness, and anguish eventually pushed her to suicide. But she never completed the job: something of her lingers still.

Certain house members swear they have heard or seen an ethereal female presence, about high school age, in the attic. One resident senses an odd, ambient hostility whenever his girlfriend is visiting. She feels it too, saying it is so intense that she will not stay alone in the room. Indeed, some members refuse to live in the attic.

Panarchy holds another disturbing secret, this one in the basement. It is one of the oddest sites you'll find anywhere on campus—the so-called "Tomb Room."

This subterranean chamber, rimmed with concrete "thrones," could be the setting for a horror film about satanic invocations.

Noting the names etched on these seats and the accompanying years (from 1897 to the 1940s) one might guess that the Tomb Room was for fraternal rites or initiations, but somehow it seems too elaborate, too expensive, and too secret for that. The "altar," a free-standing stone sarcophagus near the front, suggests darker applications. No one knows why the secret room is there, but the blood-colored candle wax splattered all over the altar sets the imagination racing. Could the "ghosts" upstairs have been conjured by unholy activities in the Tomb Room?

❧ DEATH HOUSE ❧

On February 25, 1934, the worst tragedy in Dartmouth history occurred at the Theta Chi House on North Main Street (now Alpha Theta). Everyone sleeping there—reported as nine fraternity brothers—died in their sleep. The cause: carbon monoxide leaking from the coal furnace.

Whether the building was structurally unsound or too haunted for habitation, the house was razed in 1940.

Today's Theta Chi is a different building, constructed on the old foundation. And it's there—in the basement—that spirits walk.

Even those unaware of the house's history often feel discomfort downstairs. Sometimes it's the sensation of being watched. Animals bolt from the basement. Several individuals have witnessed objects—like laundry items—move, seemingly of their own accord.

Recently I interviewed the pseudonymous Richard Caine (class of 1995), who, in the fall of 1992, had a dramatic confrontation with Theta Chi's spirits.

Richard had just joined the house. Descending into the basement for the first time, he encountered a group of strangers, perhaps ten or twelve. "Unlike the rest of us," he said, "they were all dressed very nicely." Their clothing seemed old-fashioned; the men in tuxedos, the women in ball gowns. This unfamiliar crowd was boisterously cheering the new members. "In fact," Richard said, "I couldn't hear my friend over the noise they were making."

Richard left to get a glass of water. Moments later he returned to find that all the people had vanished. Stranger still, the entire room was gone. Only a blank wall remained.

With some timidity Richard told his friend Michael DiPietro ('95) about the odd occurrence. "One of them, the loudest, was talking in an Italian accent. He sounded as if he was from New York; Brooklyn, maybe?"

Michael asked if Richard could identify their faces if he saw them again. Certain that he could, they checked the 1934 college yearbook, the Aegis. There, clearly photographed, were some of the mysterious visitors. Three had died in the 1934 gas leak.

The loudest turned out to be Americo Secondo DeMasi ('35) an Italian-American from Little Neck, New York.

The women were never identified. House belief is that they too died in the mishap. But, because they weren't allowed there in the first place, the college and families covered it up.

Odd occurrences continue in the cellar. A woman saw a disembodied face reflected in a bathroom window. People find refrigerator contents unaccountably scattered across the floor or stairs. Such manifestations are frequent enough to convince many members that the spirits of their long-dead brothers are still among them, perhaps keeping future tragedies at bay.

But the mystery remains: Why so few ghosts at Dartmouth? And why won't anyone go on record talking about them?

At Harvard, assistant dean of freshmen William C. Young met Massachusetts Hall's ghost face-to-face. He told *Harvard Magazine*, "Eighteenth-century buildings should have ghosts."

Apparently Dartmouth College should not.

Theories explaining their absence are legion and conspiracy theories more numerous still. The real answer lies with the dead, but they—like many folks at Dartmouth—aren't talking.

✃ THE SECRETS OF SAINT MICHAEL'S ✄ (A Complete Disclosure?)

In the fall of 2006 I visited Saint Michael's College in Colchester. The first thing I noticed was a baroque cross, strangely askew, high atop Founders Hall. Could it be some arcane symbol warning me that all was not right? And if so, what legends, secrets, and supernatural shenanigans might it be challenging me to discover?

Because Founders is the oldest building on campus, it seemed like the perfect place to begin looking for mysteries. I soon learned that one of the school's most unsettling terror tales is said to have happened there.

In the early 1970s a small group of students entered the building late at night and climbed quietly to the attic. There they commenced a ritual that most assuredly would be banned at any self-respecting Catholic college—they tried to summon Satan. First they drew a pentagram on the floor, and punctuated each point with a candle. Then—perhaps nervously—they began their Satanic séance.

As the evening passed, persistence seemed to pay off. Something appeared outside the window. A green, glowing ball, like a hideous head, seemed to be staring in at them. Startled by their apparent success, they did the only sensible thing: They ran away.

When word got around that this crew had had the daylights scared out of them, the Edmundite priests went up to check. In the attic they found the chalk-inscribed pentagram on the floor and quickly removed it. After a thorough treatment of prayer and holy water, they left and locked the building.

End of story?

Of course not. Repeated for decades, the story is still very much alive on campus. At one point or another, every student hears it. Can there be any substance to such an enduring tale?

❧ THE PARABLE OF THE PENTAGRAM ❧

"I think there's a lot of physical evidence
to suggest that something happened up
there that the college doesn't want to talk about."
—Brian Anderson

I first learned about the pentagram when talking with alumnus Brian Anderson, who, while a student, had worked on the paint crew and with Fire and Rescue. These activities gained him entrance to every building on campus. Over the years, patience and vigilance allowed him to piece together a more complete version of the events. Thanks to his investigative efforts we now have a fleshier version of the tale. . . and Brian has a career as an undercover investigator in federal law enforcement.

For one thing, Brian is convinced the events occurred at Joyce Hall, not Founders (nor Alumni Hall, as some students insist). There is at least one good reason to believe this: Joyce has an attic big enough to house elephants, while Founders contains only a crawlspace.

According to Brian's research, the St. Michael's students were led astray by a visiting Satanist from Burlington, Vermont. "In 1971 or '72," Brian told me. "It was an older gentleman, who got some kids interested in Satan worship and the power that it might hold."

Their sinister activities were discovered one night when a Resident Assistant (RA) heard noise in the attic where he knew nothing should be going on. He went up to investigate, "and came upon a group of students sitting in a circle, a pentagram in the middle, and candles at the points of the pentagram. The students were in some sort of trance. He recognized some, didn't recognize everybody."

Perhaps the RA didn't immediately grasp the full import of what he was seeing. "[He] broke up the event, kind of chastised everybody, sent them on their way. He didn't recognize a few, but at the time didn't take the effort to get down the names of everyone involved."

Brian says, "A pentagram had been drawn on the floor—he [the RA] kind of removed it. It was a hardwood floor. Didn't make a report of it. Just let it go."

But the story didn't end there. A few weeks later a similar event occurred. This time the RA reported it when he discovered many of the same students along with others he didn't recognize. All of them were chanting.

The RA broke up that group after taking names, but some, who were not St. Michael's students, vanished before surrendering any identifying information.

After discussing things with the Resident Director, the two decided to bring the apparent sacrilege to the attention of the campus ministry. "I think when you look at a Catholic college," Brian told me, "what are the things a Catholic College doesn't want to talk about? Devil worship would certainly be high on the list.

"In the early '70s," he continues, "the Edmundite priests played a huge role in what was going on. And they basically flipped over that issue. Some very stern warnings went out to those students."

Then, Brian says, "...the priests actually went up there. I don't think they performed an actual exorcism, but blessed the whole room. They splashed Holy Water on the spot where the pentagram had been after it was washed away. Some crosses went up in the corners of the dormitory and I believe that the attic was locked. That's the story as I recall it: that they locked it at that point and banned it from use."

But the stubborn Satanists were not so easily put off. By the time the dorms had shut down for Christmas vacation, only one person, the Resident Director, was residing in Joyce Hall.

One evening he came home to the sound of voices somewhere overhead. Since no one was supposed to be in the building, he grabbed a flashlight and headed out to investigate.

He walked from end to end of the long shadowy corridor. As he ascended another floor, the sounds got louder. When he reached the fourth floor he realized the voices were coming from the attic. Someone had smashed the lock to the attic door. Listening at the opening, he recognized chanting, but the words were unfamiliar.

The RD put in a call to security and waited. From where he stood he could tell the electric lights were turned off upstairs, but he saw the flickering of candles.

He allowed the police about fifteen minutes before climbing carefully upstairs. In the candlelight he spied a cluster of crouched figures. Shadows danced about overhead, but the stillness of the thing at the center of the pentagram scared all thought from his head.

It was a body.

A maimed sheep in a pool of blood.

A sacrifice.

The RD turned away only to be met by campus security.

This time the administration came down really hard on the students. All were expelled and escorted quietly off campus.

The incident concludes, Brian says, when "The priests went up there and really went lock, stock, and barrel: holy water everywhere. Prayers. I heard they might have been up there for 24 hours in a constant prayer vigil."

According to some versions of the story, the "Dark Knights," as the intruders have come to be called, were not in the attic to summon something. Rather, they were trying to keep something away, to close a portal between this world and some other. Perhaps that is why they stubbornly kept returning to perform their ritual at the same location—time after time—even after it had been locked up and they had been officially banished from campus.

The pentagram, whether chalked, waxed, painted, carved, or burned into the floor, stayed around to continue its dirty work. Some students say that no effort can remove it.

This grim story endures, Brian believes, because of what befell the poor students who, in subsequent years, lived beneath the pentagram. "A variety of things have happened in the room underneath where the pentagram was drawn on the floor. So much so I believe that they don't assign that room to students anymore. In fact, it's used for storage. I don't know if that's true today; I believe that was true a few years ago [when I worked at the school].

"Supposedly one or more students committed suicide. Other students suffered from migraines, inability to sleep, hearing voices, things of that nature. A few students [left] school suffering from massive depression. So the room itself got a reputation. I'm pretty sure that for a while no students lived in that room. The college didn't assign that room. And as I said, I don't know if that's still the case today."

Maybe not, but it would seem something is still up there. As recently as December 2004, fourth floor resident Deidre Kreckel (class of '08) told the online student magazine *The Echo* how, just as she was getting ready to go to bed, "The windows [in her room] were closed, but the door just opened. It's a pretty heavy door and I was freaked out. Then for an hour afterward there was just banging above me and I couldn't go to bed."

Other Joyce residents Victoria Townsend ('08) and Rachael Zimmerman ('08), say they heard constant banging from the attic. While this might be attributable to something as mundane as heating ducts, how would we explain the near constant sound of people running around overhead? "It's usually not that bad," Ms. Zimmerman said, "but some nights it's ridiculous."

When asked if anyone could corroborate his version of the Saint Michael's story, Brian Anderson thought a moment and said, "I really don't know who. The best people would be the priests [who] were there [at the time], but I know they wouldn't talk to you. I know because they won't even talk about it to people that they know."

❧ THE ARM OF SAINT EDMUND ❧

So, the clandestine activities of "The Black Knights" remain a secret—a secret society performing secret rituals at some secret time in Saint Michael's secret past.

But there are less "diabolical" mysteries to contemplate at this small Catholic school. One, quite possibly miraculous, may actually have been observed by certain of the older alumni.

Saint Michael's College was founded by the Society of Saint Edmund in 1903. And the society was founded in honor of Saint Edmund himself, a great peacemaker and the Archbishop of Canterbury who died in France on November 16, 1240. Following a spate of miracles associated with his corpse, he was canonized seven years later. Miraculously, the body remained in an excellent state of preservation for almost 800 years. It was subdivided, as saints' corpses often were. In 1954 Saint Edmund's arm was delivered as a holy relic to Saint Michael's College.

On its journey to America the middle finger of Saint Edmund's hand was accidentally broken off at the second joint. The arm was delivered to New York City for repairs, before continuing its journey to take up residence at Saint Michael's College in May, 1957.

There it rested in the old chapel in Jean Marie Hall until July 1965 when it was relocated to the Church of the Nativity of the Blessed Virgin Mary in Swanton. Today, and since December 6, 2002, the relic rests in the Chapel of Our Lady of the Assumption on Enders Island, Connecticut.

During its short stay at St. Michael's the arm may have appeared —especially to the non-Catholic students—a bit out of place, even grisly, preserved as it was in a shiny tube-like glass reliquary. Needless to say, some interesting legends grew up around it. Most notable of those recall its injured finger. According to some, the wound in the mummified hand would occasionally bleed.

As far as I can discern, this occasional blood flow did not portend anything. The seeming miracle was just visible testimony to the holiness of Saint Edmund. I guess. . .

❧ THE SAINT MICHAEL'S MASSACRE ❧

Yet visions, prophesy, and paranormal predictions are not unknown at the college.

Adam Lanthier's October, 2000 article in *The Defender*, the school newspaper, gives a great example:

In 1991, St. Michael's students were all het up about a prediction by nationally syndicated astrologer Jean Dixon. On the *Oprah Winfrey Show* Ms. Dixon foretold a terrible massacre at a small New England College. A *Catholic* college. In fact, she narrowed it down to three possible schools: Stonehill College in Massachusetts, St. Anselm's in New Hampshire, and Saint Michael's in Vermont.

The atrocity, involving the ax murder of more than 20 people, was set to occur on October 31, 1991.

News spread like an end-of-the-world announcement. Students glanced nervously over their shoulders and at each other. After sundown they scurried in tight clusters from building to building.

Later, word got out that Ms. Dixon had subsequently been slightly more specific. She said that the target school would have "round and L-shaped buildings."

Panic heightened when everyone realized that all three schools had the requisite buildings. Saint Michael's students knew that Saint Edmund's Hall is L-shaped, and, before modifications, the Durick Library was round.

The schools were on yellow alert.

The various school administrators put in calls to Oprah's producers requesting more specific information about the deadly predictions. Producers and representatives of Ms. Dixon's syndicate insisted that no such prediction had ever been aired.

Hallowe'en 1991 passed without incident.

In their collective relief no one bothered to determine just how the violent rumor had started. Well, it turns out Holy Cross went through exactly the same thing in the late 1970s.

Ms. Dixon. Ax murder massacre. Network denial. Everything. Daniel Day, editor of the Holy Cross student newspaper, published a piece debunking the threat. He discovered that even Georgetown University had experienced exactly the same scenario.

How do such terror tales migrate from one school to another? Should we blame it on the transfer students?

❧ A CAMPUS CURSE? ❧

I was surprised to find a curse story at Saint Michael's. But then again, the Bible is full of curses, so the on-site priests might be well-versed in the destructive nature of imprecations.

In 1931, an algebra class was being conducted at 9:00 a.m. on Mondays, Wednesdays, and Fridays, in room 108 of Jean Marie Hall.

One student, Michael Lavery, was chronically late for class. The repetition of his tardiness irked the professor while it amused the students. They called him "The late Mr. Lavery." So, each time he showed up for his 9:00 class at exactly 9:10, there was a double disruption: his noisy arrival and the resulting giggles and guffaws.

The priest instructor, after multiple warnings, finally reached the end of his tether. With an Irishman's verbal precision, he allegedly said, "Mr. Lavery, may the Lord keep you in Purgatory till the end of the world, and may you spend your Purgatory here, coming late to your mathematics class."

A week after being cursed, Michael Lavery actually did become "The late Mr. Lavery"; the young man inexplicably dropped dead on his way to algebra. Ever since then, professors who have used the room on Mondays, Wednesdays, and Fridays quickly discover that the door will mysteriously open and close at precisely 9:10. Regardless of the season, a cold draft will enter the room.

Although this long-ago account may be difficult to verify—especially for those looking for Room 108—the ghostly routine apparently continues.

In a November 1, 1989 issue of *The Defender*, the pseudonymous "G.H. Ostey" shared the account of a personal meeting
with "The late Mr. Lavery." At the beginning of the semester, at
exactly 9:10 a.m. on Wednesday, September 6, 1989, G.H. Ostey
was outside room 387 of Jean Marie Hall. There the writer, "…
encountered a young man dressed in a bygone style who inquired
in mournful tones where he could find room 108."

G.H. Ostey readily informed the confused specter that Room
108 had been renumbered to become 387. With a satisfied nod
the apparition turned to enter 387 and "promptly disappeared."

❧ GHOSTS GALORE ❧

The late Mr. Lavery is but one of the venerable haunts that
roam the campus.

Others include a young man who was killed after a
drunken evening when he fell down the stairs of Founders Hall.
Subsequently, on rare occasions (and perhaps inspired by more
alcohol), students have seen his ghostly free falling form reenact-
ing his death scene. Same with a student who, wearing nothing
but a top hat and a bright smile, took a dive from the roof of
Founders under the mistaken impression that he could fly. He
couldn't. But his ghost is seen at irregular intervals repeating the
attempt.

People in St. Joseph's Hall experience a spectrum of spiritual antics. One of the most memorable is the heavy concrete-
on-concrete dragging sound that is sometimes heard from the
basement. No one has been able to trace it. Brendan Kinney ('93)
recalls the time the Superior General from the Society of Saint
Edmund was visiting. He unwittingly suggested a possible explanation: When Saint Joseph's Hall was their main building, the
spot in question was where dead priests were laid out.

Then there is the building on north campus, at Fort Ethan
Allen, across from the Ellie-Long Music Center, once used as a
jail. This sturdy brown brick edifice is identifiable by prison bars
on the basement windows. Not long ago the cells down there

were used for storing luggage and other student possessions. Before that, they were used for storing military prisoners. Over the years various passersby swore they had heard crying and shouting from souls incarcerated there so very long ago.

❧ A HAUNTED HOUSE ❧

The best contender on campus for a classic haunted house is Prevel Hall. That's because it started out as a private home rather than an institutional building.

The haunting supposedly began while it was the residence of Zebulon Fisk, a rich lumber baron, who built it in 1847. Mr. Fisk had two daughters, one of whom died of a broken heart after her fiancé, a steamboat captain, drowned in Lake Champlain. Perhaps there was a component of madness in her grief because every night after his death she would compulsively climb to the rooftop's windowed room. There, lantern in hand, she waited for his return.

After her premature death, odd things began happening. Servants heard weeping in the dead girl's empty bedroom. On dark, stormy nights people would often spot a lantern behind the windows of the rooftop room.

Saint Michael's College acquired the house in 1903. It was renamed in honor of one of the Edmundite founders, Father Prevel. For years it served as a residence for the Edmundite fathers.

Miss Fisk's ghost continued to make her presence known, but she was a bit of an aberration at the all-male facility. There are even uncorroborated stories of an exorcism to help her on her way to the afterlife. If so, it was unsuccessful.

In 1950 Prevel Hall was converted into offices. Today it houses the Office of Institutional Advancement and the Office of Marketing and Communication. Employees have experienced a series of odd occurrences.

For example, Caroline Crawford, Director of Publications, has complained of a loud banging under the floor of her office.

This crashing metal sound, thunderous enough to disturb her work, could easily be tossed off as the rumbling of pipes in the cellar. Trouble is, there is no cellar under Caroline's office. And no pipes. Just floor and dirt and stones.

Brendan Kinney, director of the Saint Michael's Fund and Advancement Services, spent a number of years working in Prevel Hall where he experienced several odd occurrences. The one that most stays with him happened on a weekend during the fall of 2004 when he was driving by campus with his 4-year old son, who needed to go to the bathroom. Brendan stopped at Prevel Hall and took his boy inside. It was dark, the only illumination coming from the red "Exit" signs. The pair walked down the hallway into the west wing of the first floor. The bathroom was at the very end. While Brendan stood in the bathroom with his son, he says, "I heard a 'thunk' in the hallway. I looked out and saw that an apple that had been sitting against the wall on a shelf in the kitchen area, was suddenly sitting, stem up, in the exact middle of the hallway one or two feet away. Because I had experienced similar events while I worked in that building for eight years, I said out loud, 'It's okay, we're leaving. I'm sorry to have bothered you.'"

Patrick Gallivan, director of alumni and parent relations, had a comparable experience. Same building, same hallway, exact same spot. Late one evening while he was alone in Prevel, a garbage can lid came crashing into the middle of the hallway.

And Chris Kenney, associate athletic director, also experienced preternatural Prevel. As undergraduates he and Deb Gavron-Ravenelle were work-study students at the Sports Information Office. Chris and Deb both recall a night when they were the last to leave the building. After crossing Route 15 heading back to campus, they turned and saw a light glowing brightly in the cupola. For a moment they wondered if they were supposed to have turned it off. But they decided to forget about it and go back to their dorms. The next day while inquiring about it, Chris discovered that not only was there no light up there, but also no wiring.

Some speculate that poor Miss Fisk is still making her ever-expectant midnight rounds.

❧ SISTER SARAH ❧

The celebrity among Saint Michael's ghostly residents is, without doubt, Sister Sarah. And her kind of fame can only come from the theater.

In trying to track down her story, I was lucky enough to encounter John Coon, a 1974 graduate of the college. As a student John was involved in campus theater and later, as an equity actor, with Saint Michael's Playhouse.

John has remained part of the theater community for many years. In that time he has done a fair amount of independent research about the famous "Theater Ghost"; he even claims to have seen what might be her photograph.

John first learned the story when he was in high school, circa 1966. Later, as a college student, he did work-study at Durick Library where he had an opportunity to poke through the files. He says, "I looked at pictures and articles about what the [old theater] building was before it was brought to Saint Michael's campus after World War II. It was a cafeteria at Fort Ethan Allen. The food servers—to soldiers, and later to students—were nuns."

These were the Sisters of Saint Martha, a Canadian group who lived at Saint Michael's between 1930 and the early 1960s. They cooked, did laundry, and other tasks for the Edmundite Fathers while living in a big barrack-like convent that included the school's kitchen, theater, and dining room.

John says he discovered that "... one of the nuns passed away in her sleep one night and the bedroom where she died later on became [Professor Emeritus of Fine Arts and Playhouse producer] Donald Rathgeb's office. The nun. . . was named Sister Sarah. And that's where I believe the story had its origins. Somebody passed away in that building."

But, according to John, Sister Sarah didn't haunt that building specifically. Rather, she attached herself to the theater department itself. Consequently, after the original theater burned down, her spirit moved with the troupe too the temporary facilities of the Herrouet Theater on North Campus, and then on to the McCarthy Arts Center after its construction in the 1970s.

John Coon is convinced Sister Sarah's ghost is there to this day, but no one should be frightened of her. He says, "If you ask actors who have been in Saint Michael's Playhouse, or students during the year, during my time there, and before, and during my 13 years at the playhouse, you'll see almost every actor will say that she's a benevolent friendly ghost that follows the actors. She's not in any way evil, she's not mean. She's kind and seems like kind of a guardian with the actors."

❧ NO BODY THERE ❧

John Coon and Don Rathgeb (who's taught at the college since 1955) both tell the same story of the Herrouet Theater.

In the early '80s, student Frank Arnone—who, Don Rathgeb says, "was not a jokester or anything"—went into the theater late one night to look for Don's wife Joanne, also a theater professor.

When he heard someone on the stairs next to the ticket booth, he tried to catch up. Prof. Rathgeb explains the construction of the stairs: "The stairway up wasn't spiral, but it was about five steps up. Turn left, and five steps again. It was certainly crooked."

Before Frank reached the top, he caught a quick but certain glimpse of the back of someone's legs. He distinctly saw a long black skirt, black nylons, and black shoes.

But when he got to the floor above, no one was there. He checked the office, he checked the light booth, he checked everywhere. Nobody was around. And there was no way out.

Frank was alone in the theater. So it couldn't have been Joanne Rathgeb. Was it Sister Sarah?

❧ VICTROLA STORY ❧

John Coon had a personal confrontation with something during his freshman year, in the same general area. After dinner, and before play rehearsal, John was in the habit of sneaking into the Herrouet Theater to be alone and catch up on his homework.

He says, "About 15 minutes into studying I suddenly started hearing music coming from the light booth, which was way back in the other side of the building in the top second floor... I crept along the side of the wall till I got up to the back of the theater, got into the lobby area, went up the twisty steps that led up to the second floor. I went to the door to the booth and I distinctly heard what sounded like 1920s music, or ragtime, or Gatsby-type music. And I thought somebody might be playing a practical joke on me... I winged open the door and the music suddenly stopped, but there was an old windup Victrola sitting on a bench in the back left corner of the light booth. The turntable had been cranked and was turning. There was no record on the turntable and the needle was on the turntable itself. The needle was just scratching it as the old green felt turntable circled around and around. There was just this scratching sound. I shut off the Victrola and I left the theater and walked back up to the dormitory to wait for rehearsal to start."

❧ IT TOLLS FOR THEE ❧

In 1978 the benevolent Sister was given credit for saving the Herrouet Theater from destruction.

Late one Friday night students at a dance in the North Campus Gym, along with sleepers in nearby apartments, were disturbed by the persistent ringing of a bell. It was coming from the Base Chapel. Upon investigation, everyone saw that the Herrouet Theater, next door to the chapel, was on fire.

Someone called the fire department who quickly extinguished the blaze. Afterward, one of the firemen said, "It's really good that bell went off and people saw the fire. Otherwise it would have burned the whole building down."

He was right, but the mystery outweighs the happy ending: The chapel hadn't been used in years. It was locked up tight.

So who had sounded the alarm?

In an effort to find out, some firemen entered the chapel only to discover there was no bell rope... and no bell.

Sister Sarah to the rescue? Only she knows for sure.

❧ AND ALSO STARING … ❧

After the theater department relocated from the Herrouet to the McCarthy Arts Center, Sister Sarah continued to put in guest appearances, although many of them go uncredited. An illustrative example occurred in 1993.

A sophomore drama student was rehearsing alone on the theater stage. Suddenly, an inexplicable eerie feeling came over him. He spun around and saw a shadowy, shawl-covered figure was walking through the seats, laughing.

The student bolted. After a few strides he stopped for a reality check. When he looked back, the figure was gone.

He froze for a beat, staring open-mouthed at the empty theater. Then the figure reappeared. And the student completed his exit.

❧ THE HOLY SPIRIT ❧

One of the most poignant "sister sightings" occurred in the Chapel of Saint Michael the Archangel. It also supplies us with our most complete description of the ghostly nun.

In the summer of 1979, New York actor Larry Sharp was hired to do one show at the Playhouse theater, beginning a 17-year relationship.

In the latter part of July, during the early '90s, Larry was experiencing some difficult personal issues. So on Monday, his day off, at about 9:00 pm, he took some time out. He says, "I thought I needed to go to meditate and reflect a little bit. So I walked over to the chapel, walked in, and was just sitting… probably in the second or third pew from the back of the chapel.

"I was just reflecting, and all of a sudden I felt a presence. I turned around, and there was this nun, in a habit, standing just behind me. I nodded, and she just smiled at me, and she said, 'Larry, I want you to know that everything is going to be all right.'"

Although the black cowl on her habit made it difficult to discern facial features, Larry guessed she was in her forties. She wasn't wearing eyeglasses and he was unable to determine her hair color. "I could tell she was not overweight," Larry says. "In fact, she looked on the slim side. Her cheek bones were rather prominent, so I suspect she was rather slender. I took her to be around 5'4 or 5'5, not small, not large.

"The expression on the face was, basically... 'Beatific' would be too strong a word. It wasn't any kind of thing like a sighting of the Virgin or anything like that. It was just a very open, relaxed, calm, just matter-of-fact expression."

Larry said, "Thank you, Sister," and turned back to face the altar.

All was silent for a moment, then Larry realized it should not have been so quiet; he should have heard footsteps on the tiles. Quickly he turned around but the nun was gone.

"I thought, hmm, this is strange," Larry recalled. "So I got up and I walked out of the chapel entrance. It was dark, but I scanned left and right, I walked around the chapel and looked in that immediate area. This was within less than a minute, and I saw no one."

Larry isn't Catholic; he didn't know any nuns, yet she called him by name. How did she know his name?

Anyway, she told him everything would be all right. And for Larry, it has been.

And, thanks to that one meeting, Larry Sharp has given us the best description we have, so far, of the benevolent phantom known as Sister Sarah.

❧ LAST RIGHTS (AND WRONGS) ❧

Saint Michael's hosts many more stories like these. After all, the whole place is founded on paranormal belief. But what investigative conclusions—if any—can we draw from this brief sampling?

1. The Arm of St Edmund

The relic no longer resides on the Saint Michael's campus. Father Joseph McLaughlin assures me that the arm never bled while at St. Michael's. Subsequently, in all its years in Swanton it exhibited no miraculous behavior. Still, it boasts one seemingly supernatural quality: the ancient relic is in fact incorruptible. It's still intact while it should have turned to dust long ago.

2. *The Cursed Mr. Lavery*

Consider the cryptographic high jinx of G.H. Ostey's byline. Does the obvious pseudonym suggest false testimony or simple anonymity? Not one of the many people I interviewed at Saint Michael's was aware of the "Lavery Curse."

3. *Prevel Hall*

The sheer number of inexplicable experiences over many years suggests something paranatural is going on in Prevel Hall. Multiple witnesses, all intelligent, honest people, cannot deny the testimony of their own senses. While there has been some discussion about the ghost's identity—is it Miss Fisk or Father Prevel?—no one disagrees that weird things happen there.

Part of the legend is that at one point occurrences became so disruptive that employees had to call in one of the Edmundite Fathers to perform an exorcism. Some people say they almost remember the event; others say they can identify the priest involved. It was Father Tom Hoar, who later left his post at St. Michael's to become an administrator on Saint Edmund's Ender's Island in Mystic Connecticut. I contacted Father Hoar, who, according to the island's newsletter, possesses excellent "Hoar's Sense." He explained that the Rite of Exorcism was never performed at Prevel. What people remember was in fact a routine blessing, one used any time new people occupy a new building. The same thing would have occurred had there been no reports of anomalous phenomena.

4. *The Saga of Sister Sarah*

This story has a lot of traction. There have been multiple witnesses over several decades, beginning, so it would seem, sometimes in the 1960s. There is enough continuity among sightings, and enough harmony among believers that we can categorize the story of Sister Sarah as, at least conditionally, true. Of course with ghosts there can never be any conclusive proof. Belief, after all, is a choice. If we decide it is true, then it's true. Sister Sarah is as faith-based as the Catholic Church itself.

5. *The Diabolical Pentangle*

Without doubt this saga of demonic antics and exorcism is Saint Michael's most unsettling "weird tale."

Although the story has been floating around the campus for years, it remains impervious to verification. All accounts say that it took place in the "early 1970s." I can find no indication that it occurred prior to that, and no valid indication that it occurred after. No one has been able to identify any of the people allegedly involved. We don't have one single name. So we can't pinpoint exactly what year it took place, who was present, or exactly what supposedly occurred. The tale appears to be an urban legend, a typical friend-of-a-friend story, used as "privileged information" to "gain rank" over first year students in Joyce Hall.

The attic of Joyce is gigantic, but it is double-locked and no one can get up there without proper keys. Exactly how students can assert "the pentagram is still there" is a mystery. Although some claim to have seen it, such declarations, even if true, fail to support the whole story. One graduate said it was carved into the "wooden" floor. This is unlikely because on September 8, 2006, Rick Battistoni, a Saint Michael's administrator and I ventured into Joyce's mysterious attic. The floor is not wooden, it's concrete, or something very like it (a substance used in these vintage 1960 buildings to retard fire). With high powered flashlights Rick and I searched every inch of that vast expanse of floor. We found no trace of anything that could be mistaken for a Pentagram.

In the final analysis, I think the dates of the Pentagram story are significant. The time parallels an event that had indelible cultural impact in the "early '70s." In 1971 *The Exorcist*, William Peter Blatty's bestselling novel of demonic possession was published. In 1973 William Friedkin's blockbuster film adaptation hit the screen. Set in and around a Catholic school, Georgetown University, it seems only natural that St. Michael's would adapt its own variation of the tale.

Both stories have had real staying power.

❧ AFTERWORD: A FINAL MYSTERY ❧

I was never able to put the pentagram story to bed. Since I explored the attic in 2006 I have repeatedly run into people who say the story is true and that the pentagram is, in fact, there.

Finally, in 2011, my friend Jeff Stewart told me he had personally seen the pentagram.

No way, I thought. I had been up there. I'd examined every inch of that floor. There were no satanic markings anywhere to be found.

Jeff, the founder of Paranormal Investigators of New England, is as skeptical as I am and as honest as anyone I know. If Jeff said he'd seen the pentagram I had no choice but to believe him. Still, as President Reagan used to say, "Trust, but verify." Jeff and I planned to venture into Joyce's attic; I wanted to see for myself.

In 2009 Jeff had been admitted to the Joyce attic by an acquaintance who worked at the college. The same acquaintance agreed to let Jeff and me take another look.

January 14, 2011 was a cold winter night. School was not in session. The buildings were locked. The campus seemed empty.

Jeff and I waited outside for his contact with the key. He was late and we were cold, but after he arrived, things happened very quickly. He let us into the building and led up to the locked room on the top floor that contained a ladder to the attic. The hatch was double locked, but our contact person quickly unlocked everything and vanished, leaving Jeff and me to our fate.

We ascended the steep metal ladder and, for the second time in my life, I climbed into that immense, dark, legend laden space.

It was exactly as I remembered, vast, poorly lighted, and barren. Each of us was armed with a powerful flashlight.

I trust Jeff completely, but a nagging tickle in the back of my mind kept saying we were on a wild goose chase.

After a few minutes of searching Jeff said, "Here, look at this."

I crossed the floor and stared down into the brightly illuminated circle of his flashlight beam. At first it was impossible to make anything out against the dark, dusty floor. But as we studied the area things became easier to discern. There were faint lines on the floor, perfectly straight as if drawn with a ruler. They were scuffed out in places, but our imaginations could fill in the blanks. First, there was a faint layer of what appeared to be red chalk. On top of it, in some places, we could make out a thin bead of red wax. Five tiny pools of wax marked the five points of what indeed was a ten-foot pentagram. It was there. We were even able to photograph parts of it.

Could it have survived there since the early 1970s?

Hard to believe. And, frankly, I don't see how I could have missed it when I examined the floor in 2006.

The fact that we found beer cans and cigarette butts near the diagram suggested it might have been made between 2006 and 2011.

Had someone gained access to Joyce's attic and planted clues to reinforce the school's favorite legend? Were people currently coming here to dabble in the satanic arts? Or had the nearly invisible marking survived there since the days of the "Dark Knights"?

There's simply no way to tell, but for now this most unsettling of Saint Michael's Mysteries lives on.

☙ WEIRD WOODSTOCK: TOWN FOR TOURISTS, HOME FOR GHOSTS ❧

*People come to this Vermont town
to step out of the present and into
the past. And vice versa.*

Question: What do Melvin Douglas, Fred Astaire, and Douglas Fairbanks Jr. have in common?

Answer: They all appeared in the movie *Ghost Story*, filmed partly in Woodstock. Of course, that harrowing tale was fiction, based on Peter Straub's classic supernatural novel. But here's what's true: Woodstock in a great place for ghosts.

Influential local farmer Gaius P. Cobb believed it. In 1851 he built a rapping machine designed so local folks could dialog with ghosts. "It had 36 keys like a Piano, 26 letters & 10 figures, so that the Spirits could communicate by rapping one and then another...." That's how Mr. Cobb's son Charles described it. The machine itself has vanished. But Woodstock ghosts seem to communicate very well without mechanical assistance. They'll reach out to you—unpredictably—in many venerable locations around town.

After Polly Billings bought F.H Gillingham & Sons general store in 1970, she often spent time there after hours, in the oldest part of the building, alone. "I never felt as if I was by myself," she says. "It was as if F.H. was right there with me. When I couldn't get an idea for the advertising copy, he would often help me out." Thing is, her "helper" died back in 1918.

The Dana House, headquarters of the Woodstock Historical Society, is a longtime habitat for haunts. Constructed in 1808, it has been accumulating spectral residents for two centuries.

Its Victorian Parlor seems to be the spiritual hotspot. There dozens of people have seen a woman wearing a long, brown, satin dress. Sometimes she will look directly at the startled witness. Sometimes she'll remain invisible, playing the piano. Former Historical Society director Corwin Sharp recalls comforting a volunteer who'd had a meeting with the Victorian specter. "She wasn't making it up," he told me. "She was shaken, white as a ghost herself."

A little boy is occasionally spotted on the stairs. He seems to be about two years old and is presumed to be the ectoplasmic residue of Mary and Charles Dana's first born, who died at the age of two. Staff and visitors frequently encounter this strange pair. They are easily recognized because of their anachronistic attire. And because they vanish before your eyes.

Another beautiful brick colonial house near The Green, and not far from the covered bridge, has a reputation for being permanently occupied, even when vacant. Historically, tenants have moved in and left quickly.

Maybe it's the heating bills. One former renter told me they could never get the place above 65 degrees, no matter how much fuel they burned. What they lost on heating costs they saved in air conditioning bills.

A more tangible occurrence convinced the family they were living with ghosts. They'd come home to find pictures from the walls smashed. Sometimes the doorknob in the master bedroom would turn of its own accord. On other occasions the door would open and close, though no one was there.

Once, while home alone, the couple heard a loud crash from above. They ran upstairs to find a precious Civil War era engraving in pieces on the far side of the room.

They moved out before knowing who their ghost was or how they had provoked its interest. Later, they learned a story connected with their former residence. Seems the house had once been a school in which the lovely young teacher had been murdered by a pale, thin, blond-headed soldier.

Maybe so, maybe not.

Perhaps we can learn the answer in court.

Certainly the Windsor County Court House is an emotional battery. Highly charged testimony, even death sentences, have been stored within its walls since 1855. Custodial staff working alone in the building report footsteps, unfathomable utterances, and awful noises. Sometimes, while court is in session, the door to the Judge's Room will open and close. Moments later, the Witness Room door on the far side of the room will rattle, just as if something invisible had crossed the courtroom from one door to the other. A judge who witnessed the phenomenon from the bench looked over at the sheriff and said, "Ghosts."

I guess that's the official verdict.

The bottom line is, we don't know for sure; ghosts might not be real. But ghost stories are. And Woodstock is effervescent with them. They even appear on the web. Ghosts of America, which calls itself, "The Scariest Site in the Country," tells about the phantom planter, wearing a straw hat, who sometimes appears at the stroke of midnight at the Billings Farm Museum. Apparently he's weeping. How anyone can identify tears at that hour is part of the mystery. As the website states, "The witness was terrified and ran away. No matter what folks exclaim, this ghost unquestionably is frightening; one that should be avoided."

Lunkheaded stories like this show how difficult it is to fillet fact from fiction in the uncertain supernatural realm. Misperception, hoaxing, and lies forever compete with honest testimony and hardcore facts. Especially vexing are the incidents when the witness is all alone, allowing no corroborating statements. Sometimes the evidence itself vanishes along with the ghost, as in this baffling tale of a Woodstock cemetery.

A deer hunter recalls the afternoon he got lost in the woods near Woodstock. Mounting darkness and falling snow made it nearly impossible to see. Wandering blindly, he eventually came to a rock wall, so he followed it downhill until it opened onto an ancient, unkempt cemetery.

He shuddered. What if he had to spend the night here? How

ironic to freeze to death in a cemetery. Just as his panic peaked, he heard a woman singing. Squinting into the blinding snowfall, he could vaguely see her, wearing a white nightdress. She had no coat, no blanket, nothing to protect her from the storm. A shawl around her head concealed her features.

He spoke, but she did not reply. Instead, she lifted her left hand, pointing. He is sure she said a single word: "There." He looked, turned back, and she was gone. No footprints marked the snow where she had stood.

More puzzled than ever, he began walking in the direction she had indicated. Soon he came to a road which led him downhill. When he saw the lights of a farmhouse he ran to the door and knocked. The farmer welcomed him with food and coffee by a snug fire. Slowly he relaxed enough to tell everyone what had happened to him. The family remained strangely silent.

Later, as the farmer drove him home, an uncomfortable silence filled the cab of the pickup. Finally, in a low voice, the farmer told the hunter that he shouldn't tell stories like that; they upset people. He said, There's no cemetery back in those woods, and never has been.

Months later, with the snow gone and the ground solid, the hunter went back to see for himself. He tried to revisit the spot and to find the graveyard or rock wall. They were not in the woods, not on any map, not listed in any of the town records.

That graveyard, like the phantom who saved the hunter's life, is only a sampling of the myriad ghosts of Woodstock.

❧ SECTION III. ❧
ODDBALLS AND ODDITIES

Some people say you can define Vermont by the character of its people. In this section we'll define Vermont by its characters, people who live a little outside the constraints of normality. Some might call them kooks, eccentrics, oddballs, or worse. Here in Vermont we just call them neighbors.

ᴥ BROOKLINE'S MAN OF MYSTERY ᴦ

If you're ever prowling the back roads of southern Vermont and happen to drift a little off course near Newfane, you might pass through the hard-to-find village of Brookline.

If you do, you'll see a legitimate local curiosity: a round schoolhouse. It may be the only one in the country. This truncated silo is made of brick with five windows evenly spaced around the perimeter.

Its designer is famous—perhaps infamous—but not as an architect. Dr. John Wilson is remembered as a genuine man of mystery.

He appeared in Newfane in 1821. No one was sure where he came from, but he definitely wasn't local. Over six feet tall and elegant, he spoke with the refined accent of an educated Scotsman. The doctor was always poised, finely dressed, and toted a walking stick.

He said he was a physician and surgeon, but offered his services as an educator. To the locals he was a gift from Heaven: doctor and schoolteacher combined, for a single, reasonable wage. His only condition was that he be allowed to design his academy.

In 1822 the schoolhouse was built to his specifications where it remains to this day. But almost 200 hundred years later we're still asking the same question: Why round?

Other questions began almost at once. Locals couldn't figure out why their aristocratic educator would accept a position as a lowly schoolmaster. And why in such a tiny, out-of-the-way place? His medical skills could earn him a fortune in bigger cities like Brattleboro or Burlington.

Dr. Wilson's behavior was an ongoing puzzle. He was friendly enough, in a standoffish sort of way. Although clearly brilliant and eloquent, he could never be coaxed into talking about his past in the British Isles.

Some people noticed that he occasionally—but only occasionally—walked with a slight limp. Others questioned why he always wore high collars or thick scarves when neither fashion nor temperature required them.

Ladies couldn't fail to notice the handsome newcomer. Yet, despite their flirtations, brazen or subdued, he unfailingly retained an impersonal distance.

After a year of teaching, Dr. Wilson resigned his post to hang up his medical shingle in nearby Newfane. There he practiced for twelve years. Patients flocked from distant towns, but he remained a loner, acquiring acquaintances rather than friends.

Then one day, without warning, he up and moved to Brattleboro.

Around 1836 the doctor married a local lass named Miss Chamberlain. Their union ended in less than two years. Neither party would explain why they had separated. Some said it was the doctor's taste for alcohol; others suspected the bride had learned something about her husband that frightened her away.

Thereafter, Dr. Wilson became even more of a recluse, careless about his grooming, and apparently unemployed. But he was never forgotten; people continued to ask questions about the mysterious aristocratic gentleman they had once called teacher and doctor.

Answers didn't come until May of 1847. As Dr. Wilson lay dying he summoned his closest friend—a man who had never pried into his affairs—and implored him to oversee final arrangements. Dr. Wilson wanted to be buried just as he was, in the cloths he was wearing—including his high scarf and leather boots. "You must also promise," he said, "to destroy everything that I own."

Luckily for collectors of Vermont mysteries, the friend ignored Dr. Wilson's dying wishes. While undressing the corpse, the undertaker discovered a cork prosthesis where Dr. Wilson's heel had been shot away. The nasty scar of a musket ball marred his withered leg, a leg that had been padded with paper and cloth to make it appear undamaged. And, beneath the scarf, Dr. Wilson's neck was horribly disfigured, as if he had been slashed, shackled, or unsuccessfully hanged. Someone discovered a stiletto concealed in the walking-stick he always carried. An examination of his home revealed a veritable arsenal of swords, guns, and ammunition.

So who was this mystery man who had lived among them, aiding, but never really integrating into their community?

Flashback to 1821. While Dr. Wilson was arriving in Vermont's West River Valley, a man named Michael Martin was hanged for highway robbery in Boston. Before he died, Mr. Martin penned his "confessions." His lurid account of daring do in the British Isles was widely read. There, due to his swiftness, Michael Martin had been known as "Lightfoot." His partner in crime, the Edinburgh-educated John Doherty, was known as "Captain Thunderbolt." For over a decade the pair had terrorized the Irish countryside and the England-Scotland border. Then they fled to America and went their separate ways.

Apparently some local scholar in Brookline, Newfane, or Brattleboro had read *Lightfoot and Thunderbolt: The Confession of Michael Martin* and noticed the similarities between the dashing Captain Thunderbolt and retiring Doctor Wilson.

The physical descriptions matched exactly, right down to the position of wounds and the withered leg.

The conclusion seemed inescapable: Brookline's reclusive schoolmaster was none other than the infamous British highwayman. Known as a swashbuckling Robin Hood-like rogue, Captain Thunderbolt was reputed to have robbed from the rich, given to the poor, and stashed away enough to escape to the wilds of America. There, hiding in rural Vermont, he became a model citizen. But he never stopped peering warily in all directions from the windows of his lookout—Brookline's round, brick schoolhouse.

The fascinating story of Captain Thunderbolt may sound like fiction, but it can be easily verified. The round schoolhouse still stands. Dr. Wilson's grave is in Brattleboro's Prospect Hill Cemetery. Copies of Michael Martin's pamphlet—originals and reprints— can be found in many Vermont libraries. And if you're still not convinced, just drop by the Brooks Library in Brattleboro. Their Vermont Room displays some of Dr. Wilson's possessions, among them his false heel, his medical instruments, his photograph, and his potentially lethal sword cane.

❧ THE MAN WHO PLAYED DETECTIVE ❧

"But look at these lonely houses, each in its own field....
Think of... the hidden wickedness which may go on,
year in, year out, in such places, and none the wiser."
—Sherlock Holmes

For a period of sixteen years, Vermont's quaint and quiet town of Chester was terrorized by a phantom.

In the beginning his thievery might have gone unnoticed— a misplaced pocket watch, a vanished dinnerpail, some missing linen—so it is difficult to pinpoint precisely when the crime wave began. But stark certainty displaced ambiguity one September night in 1886 with a safecracking at the Adams and Davis Company.

Before reeling citizens could recover their equilibrium, other crimes followed, but they were odd, seemingly motiveless, with no discernible pattern. The phantom made off with a box of bow ties, a bag of donuts, roofing shingles, sacks of grain—all from different Chester merchants. On the night of April 30, 1894 he smashed a window at Charles Walker's Furniture Store. The fancy new "safety bicycle" it had displayed—the kind where both wheels are the same size—was missing in the morning.

But the burglaries' near-whimsical tone changed when farmer George Allen and his wife were rudely awakened by a masked bandit standing at the foot of their bed. Pointing a revolver at them, he said he had an associate waiting outside who would shoot them dead if they left the house before daylight.

The bandit—or possibly bandits—ransacked the house and made off with $1500 in cash that Mr. Allen had recently received from a cattle sale.

Constable Henry Bond surmised the thief must be known to the family, otherwise their dog would have warned them of the intruders. Soon after, he discovered the animal's poisoned corpse.

Mr. Bond quickly organized a posse. They searched the area and blocked roads leading out of town, but the phantom had vanished.

At this point the domestic tranquility of Chester was severely disturbed. None of its 2000 residents felt safe. Strangers were regarded with an unfamiliar distrust, neighbors—for the first time—looked at each other with suspicion. Formerly relaxed townsfolk took to bolting their doors and sleeping with firearms at their bedsides.

Though various security measures were taken, the thefts continued, almost on a weekly basis. They were consistently unpredictable and seemingly senseless—two qualities that made Chester's phantom especially terrifying.

Neighboring communities were sometimes victimized, but most of the crimes occurred in Chester, giving credence to the uncomfortable suspicion that the phantom might be one of their own.

Adding insult to injury, his—or her—escapades seemed to demonstrate a perverse contempt for the victims and for the law. The phantom would never take the easy route into a building if a complicated one were available. The actions indicated great strength, agility, and apparently a sinister, cunning, intelligence. No one, nothing, was safe from Chester's ingenious and eclectic thief.

> *"I have enjoyed the distinction and*
> *have prized dearly the compliment*
> *of being a conspicuous citizen."*
> —Clarence Adams

In those days Vermont had no state police force. Crime fighting—what there was of it—was the responsibility of the constable and the Board of Selectmen.

The citizens of Chester considered themselves lucky to have as their first selectman the distinguished Mr. Clarence Adams. Though born in neighboring Cavendish in 1857, Mr. Adams had grown up in Chester and—even as a lad—had demonstrated exceptional intelligence, wisdom, and diplomacy. In adolescence he had talked about a career in the military. Later he considered detective work or the secret service. But he won the respect of his neighbors when he chose to remain on the isolated family farm, tending the business and taking care of his aging, ailing parents.

When they passed on, Clarence continued working his 270-acres and buried himself in the affairs of the town. He was deacon at the local church, a founding trustee of the Whiting Library, a village lister, and an incorporator of the Chester Savings Bank. In time his interests turned to politics. He was elected First Selectman in 1892—a position roughly equivalent to mayor—and even represented Chester in the Vermont legislature.

At six feet tall, the well-groomed, blue-eyed, and mustachioed Mr. Adams was considered handsome. Farm work kept him healthy; reading kept him well-informed and cultured. His personal library included nearly 2000 volumes.

Though he avoided small talk, Mr. Adams was well-spoken, with a good word for everyone. As Ed Kendall recalled in 1955, "It was a pleasure to listen to him as he took part in town meeting debates."

In short, he was the sort of man who won the respect of his peers, turned the heads of the ladies, and inspired mothers to cite him as a role model for their sons. His only "vice," folks said, was too much reading. Rather than spin yarns and swap gossip at the general store, he'd invariably return to his farm on the hill and the solitude of his library. But everyone had to admit that self-education had made him the most learned man in town. They even entrusted him as the unofficial guardian of juvenile morals by having him select all the books for the town library.

So when Mr. Adams decided to take a personal interest in the burglaries, most people breathed a sigh of relief. The voracious reading they'd teased him about might prove to be their salvation. Mr. Adams admitted to a special fondness for detective fiction. He read police thrillers of the era, including Nick Carter and "Old Sleuth," but he admired the works of Poe, Gaboriau, and especially Conan Doyle's Sherlock Holmes stories.

No doubt his fellow selectmen chided him a bit when they saw how eager Clarence was to put his own sleuthing skills to work. Clearly, he wanted to play detective.

Not surprisingly, the multi-talented Mr. Adams displayed an aptitude for police work. Before long he was running the investigation. He approved security plans, consulted about strategy, questioned victims, even examined crime scenes, often disclosing the burglar's ingenious mode of entry.

Everyone—even Constable Bond—felt better now that Mr. Adams was on the case.

Together the selectmen made a number of decisions: Clarence suggested they hire a professional detective from Boston to investigate the crimes; they'd find an assistant for poor Constable Bond, who admitted he was baffled by the whole troubling mess; and they'd post a $500 reward.

Again Mr. Adams reinforced people's confidence by adding another $100 of his own money.

He suggested that druggist F.W. Pierce purchase a supply of revolvers to sell to frightened citizens. And he personally helped James E. Pollard's plan to install a burglar alarm system at his general store. The place had been hit at least six times and Mr. Pollard was at wits' end.

Also, on his way home, Mr. Adams routinely stopped at the grist mill to pass the time of day with his friend Charles Waterman. Mr. Waterman's Mill had been robbed at least sixteen times—more than any other business—and Clarence readily offered support and consolation. In time he convinced the frugal Mr. Waterman that it would be cost effective to employ a night watchman.

But as usual, the phantom was one step ahead of his pursuers. Before Druggist Pierce's revolvers were sold, they were stolen.

As if to mock Mr. Pollard's high-tech security system, the thief somehow broke in without triggering the alarm, then left with a fur coat, a woman's cape, and fifteen dollars. Upon investigation, Clarence Adams discovered how the theft had been accomplished. The thief had entered through a 14 by 18 inch closet window, the only one not wired because it was considered too small and too high up to be accessible.

And Waterman's Mill was robbed on the watchman's night off.

In time nearly every store in Chester, the post office, the railroad station, and many private homes, were burgled. Often the method of entry could not be detected. It was as if the mysterious thief truly were a phantom.

Or a phantom with a set of keys.

By now people were thoroughly convinced the villain was a fellow townsman. Distrust and suspicion rose to a point never equaled before or since.

The selectmen's action brought about some promising developments. For example, their hired detective identified a couple of suspects. Then, upon discovering a source of illegal alcohol in the temperate town, the sloshed sleuth quickly got himself fired.

One suspect, a local ne'er-do-well named Gideon Lee, was arrested, but there simply wasn't enough evidence to convict. He lived under the disreputable stigma until he died, but even then the burglaries continued.

Thomas Converse also became a suspect after he was arrested for robbery elsewhere in Windsor County. He was sent to the jail in Woodstock where he soon passed away, all the while protesting his innocence.

Yet the burglaries didn't stop.

Now even Clarence Adams admitted he was baffled.

"When you have eliminated the impossible,
whatever remains, however improbable,
must be the truth."
—Sherlock Holmes

മ ൜

Charles H. Waterman had been cogitating some on the whole maddening affair. Because his mill was the thief's most frequent target, Mr. Waterman took the intrusions very personally.

Each time he had been burgled he and Clarence Adams had determined the point of entry and had secured it so as to make a second break-in impossible.

But knowing the thief's penchant for the impossible, Mr. Waterman guessed a single window over the river would be the phantom's next port of entry. There he and his 20-year-old son Gardner constructed an apparatus—a system of strings and pulleys—that would squeeze the trigger of a shotgun the moment the window was opened. Mr. Waterman had no intention of killing the thief; he filled the gun with birdshot and aimed it low, intending it to strike the leg or foot of any would-be intruder.

He was eager to show his invention to Clarence, but Clarence was away on business. Pleased as he was with his Yankee ingenuity, Mr. Waterman dared not show his booby-trap to anyone else.

On the night of July 29, 1902, Charles Waterman attended a school board meeting at the nearby town hall, leaving his son Gardner at home.

Around 9:30 there was an explosion.

At about 10:00 Clarence Adams pounded on the door to his home. When it opened he fell into the arms of his elderly housekeeper, Mrs. Elmina Walker.

"Quickly," he said, "send for Doctor Havens. I've been shot."

His friend Will Dunn, who was visiting at the time, helped Mrs. Walker carry Clarence to a bed.

"Who shot you, Clarence?" Will asked.

"The burglar," Clarence said. "He stopped me down at the foot of the hill. Shot me. Took my money. Left me for dead."

"Did you see who—?"

"Masked. He—they—wore masks."

At the same time young Gardner Waterman raced to the

town hall to fetch his father and Constable Bond. With great caution the trio explored the inside of the mill. Lantern light revealed the broken window and bloody shards of glass.

Shortly, the constable was summoned from the mill. Along with Dr. Walter Havens, they raced to the Adams farmhouse. As Constable Bond listened to Clarence's story, Dr. Havens examined his mutilated leg. It was a nasty wound; the doctor thought recovery unlikely.

Word quickly spread that there had been two crimes that night in Chester: the Waterman robbery and the Adams shooting. The violence was especially troubling; it was a first. Folks speculated Clarence was getting too close to the thief's identity.

Meanwhile Constable Bond went about his plodding business. He rechecked the mill and discovered the first substantial clue to the phantom's identity: the Number 8 shot fired from Mr. Waterman's gun matched exactly the 84 pieces of buckshot removed from Clarence Adams's leg.

His conclusion, though impossible to believe, was inescapable: Clarence Adams and Chester's Phantom Burglar were one and the same.

Armed with a warrant, the disbelieving Constable searched the Adams house and property. There he discovered evidence of Clarence Adams's dark half. His library was nearly half full of crime and adventure books. Conspicuous too were occult volumes, the works of Anton Mesmer (a pioneer in the science of hypnotism), and, ironically, a well-worn copy of Robert Louis Stevenson's Doctor Jekyll and Mr. Hyde.

They also found boxes of bow ties, bundles of shingles, guns, jewelry, fine women's clothing, a "burglar's kit," and, hanging out back in a tree, a rusted twin-wheeled bicycle.

Clarence Adams had no choice but to confess. What he said may be the nearest thing we'll ever have to a motive for his extraordinary crimes. He testified that he had developed both sides of his nature, encouraging the good as well as the bad. It had worked: he'd become the town's leading citizen and the most wanted criminal in the state.

"Yet... I have even more
keenly enjoyed the indulgence
of my criminal instincts....
I have indulged both my duel
personalities—I have encouraged
my honorable ambitions and my
dishonorable ones."

—Clarence Adams

About two weeks later, on August 14, 1902, the still-recovering Clarence was carried on a chair up the narrow, twisting stairs to the Windsor Country Courthouse in Woodstock.

Judge Seneca Haselton sentenced him to 10 years hard labor at Windsor prison.

Behind bars, his education, poise, and cunning made him an ideal prisoner. He quickly became the prison librarian and somehow charmed Warden E. W. Oakes, perhaps by donating so many of his own books to the prison library. Mostly, Clarence kept to himself, but he did befriend another inmate, an educated man who'd had some medical training. Clarence Adams's new friend worked as an orderly, assisting the prison's consulting physician, Dr. John D. Brewster.

An occasional visitor broke the monotony of Clarence's prison life, the most frequent being his good friend, William Dunn. Then, on February 22, 1904, Clarence Adams took sick. A pneumonia epidemic was in progress, so Dr. Brewster and his orderly had their hands full.

Every day Clarence's condition worsened. Dr. Brewster ordered him moved to the prison infirmary where he was tended by his friend. Convinced his time would soon be up, Clarence requested that Warden Oakes release his remains to his friend Will Dunn.

On Friday, February 26, 1904, Clarence Adams died. His friend the orderly prepared the death certificate which Dr. Brewster—perhaps after a perfunctory reading—signed. Cause of death: "oedema of the lungs"—pneumonia.

And this is where the story of Chester's leading citizen—and Vermont's public enemy number one—should end.

But it doesn't. In April, about a month after Clarence Adams's death, people started seeing him. Not his ghost, but the real flesh and blood Clarence.

A local salesman, John Greenwood—"a man whose word has never been questioned and who has known Adams for many years" —spoke with him in Montreal. Another traveler saw him in Nova Scotia. Much later, people ran into him out west....

It seemed Chester's Phantom had somehow returned from the dead.

A lurid but fascinating theory was posed in the Boston newspapers, then echoed in papers all over the world. They argued that Clarence Adams might be as clever breaking out of places as he was breaking in.

Had he, they asked, engineered an ingenious escape from jail? If so, how?

In 1929 Edward H. Smith published a book called You Can Escape in which he scrutinizes the Clarence Adams story. If Mr. Smith's hypothesis is true, it is remotely possible that Clarence read the book himself.

Edward Smith claims to have information from a man who was incarcerated in Windsor at the same time as Clarence Adams. From this unidentified ex-con we learn the "prison version" of the story. The escape, he said, required $3000, the cooperation of an outsider (presumably Will Dunn) and the help of the inmate-physician.

From this point on, facts and speculation frequently mesh as we try to reconstruct Clarence Adams's death, resurrection, and escape. As with all great mysteries, for every fact there is a question:

Fact: Clarence Adams was a student of the arcane and the occult.

He was allegedly able to hypnotize himself. In fact, one of his books on "Mesmerism" is now in the possession of the Chester Historical Society.

Question: Could he have put himself into a hypnotic sleep and passed himself off as dead?

Fact: The official prison doctor, Dr. Brewster, never examined the corpse.

Question: Did Clarence Adams's orderly friend, a co-conspirator, get the death certificate quickly signed by the overworked Dr. Brewster?

Fact: William Dunn, along with a coffin, arrived Saturday morning to claim the body without having been summoned or informed that Adams had died.

Question: Could his arrival have been arranged well in advance?

Fact: Will Dunn took possession of Adams's remains and helped mortician Lyman Cabot transport the corpse to his Windsor undertaking establishment where it lay unattended all Saturday afternoon.

Question: Is it possible that somewhere between the jail and the embalming process, Clarence's body was switched for a cadaver, perhaps obtained from the nearby Dartmouth Medical School? Our "prison informer" says that's what part of the $3000 was for.

Fact: On Monday a casket—ostensibly Clarence's—was transported 25 miles to the Cavendish cemetery where it was stored in the vault until the ground was soft enough for burial.

Question: Who, or what, was in the coffin?

Fact: No family member ever identified the body. But cemetery sexton Henry D. Sanders opened the box and peeked at the corpse. "It looked like Clarence," he said.

Question: But was it? After two months in a box, wouldn't anyone look like Clarence? And was there any reason to believe Mr. Sanders knew what Clarence looked like?

Fact: Suddenly Henry D. Sanders was able to pay off most of his debts.

Question: Isn't the acquisition of this sudden wealth rather oddly timed?

Fact: Reliable witnesses claimed to have seen and talked to

Clarence after his supposed "death." John Greenwood, a respected salesman for Dunham Brothers of Brattleboro, said he had met and chatted with Clarence in the lobby of the Hotel Windsor in Montreal.

The question is obvious, as is Mr. Adams's sense of irony in his choice of hotel.

Fact: The family never permitted the grave to be opened to determine who—or what—the casket contains.

Question: Why not?

Put these facts and possibilities together and it looks as if Mr. Adams engineered a shrewd escape from prison and from the tomb.

But someone's body remained in the Cavendish vault until the ground was soft enough for it to be buried on May 1, 1904.

Was it Clarence Adams? Can we ever find out for sure?

If the coffin were inspected now, more than a century after burial, the condition of the corpse would make identification impossible. There would be no fingerprints, no dental records, no DNA certainty.

But there is a way to tell. Although Clarence Adams's flesh may be entirely gone, one thing would not decompose: number 8 shot from the gunshot wound. Wayne Dengler, former investigator for the Windham County State's Attorney, and Rick Bates, Windham Country Superintendent of the Vermont Department of Corrections, tell me there is no way Dr. Havens could have removed all the shot. There would probably be a good teaspoonful in the casket. Also, Adams's leg bone would be pitted in a telltale manner.

Today the town of Chester remains divided as to the fate of its most infamous native son. There is no question about his 16-year reign of terror, no doubt about his incarceration at Windsor Prison, but as to his death and resurrection? Students of this bizarre bit of Vermontiana can't seem to agree.

Chris Curran, former President of the Chester Historical Society, recently reviewed the case to assist with a Japanese television documentary. He says, "It seems altogether plausible from his modus operandi that he very well could have pulled off a fake death and escaped from prison."

Jack Coleman, retired college president and former Chester innkeeper, researched the case for his play, "The Ballad of Clarence Adams." When asked about the Chester Burglar's fate, he replies without hesitation, "I think he escaped. I don't have any doubt in my mind at all."

But the only real proof is in the ground, and the only way to bring it to light is with a shovel.

So far, that hasn't happened. The truth is quite literally "buried" and the legend is still very much alive.

❧ THE PERFECT VERMONTER ❧

Vermont has a way of inspiring wildly unconventional religious notions. There was the prophet Joseph Smith, Priest Wood and his talking stick, William Miller with his doomsday predictions, Melissa Warner and her floating deities. The list goes on and on.

But of the many contenders for Vermonters' souls, my favorite by far is John Humphrey Noyes.

Born in Brattleboro on September 3, 1811, John came from a strict Protestant farm family. He was Dartmouth educated and religiously driven. Much of his youth was spent trying to overcome a curse: what the Noyeses referred to as "the family affliction." John, and other Noyes men, suffered from a paralyzing shyness around women.

His solution was extreme, far-reaching, and more than a little X-rated.

He began his professional career as a practicing lawyer, which permitted him to sharpen his thinking skills and powers of persuasion. He began to question his religious upbringing and, briefly, even flirted with agnosticism.

But the imprint of his childhood religious indoctrination was too strong. In 1831 a "revelation" of some sort led him back to the church and on to Andover Seminary where he became a member of a secret society of students called The Brethren. After a year at Andover the young zealot answered a higher calling: Yale

Divinity School. There he set his mind to Bible study. Somehow he was able to compute the exact date of Christ's second coming. This led to another revelation: Christ had already arrived. Way back in 70 A.D.

It only stood to reason, John thought, that if the reign of Christ had already begun then he and other "true believers" were living without sin and should be permitted, while on earth, to enjoy all the perquisites of the heavenly state.

He preached this unusual doctrine to his new congregation: Everyone was released from sin. There was no such thing as damnation. And humankind's only job was to attain Perfection.

All this unorthodoxy was a little uncomfortable for his superiors, his congregation, and the professors and students at Yale. After all, the man considered himself "a perfect saint." Such self-aggrandizement led some to think that Rev. Noyes ought to be tried for heresy, not because he was bad but because he thought himself so good.

No trial resulted, but John's preaching license was revoked.

Another "dark night of the soul" soon followed: the woman he loved rejected him, reinforcing the idea of a family curse.

Wounded, but still "perfect," John relocated to Putney, Vermont where he began to put his "Perfectionism" plans into motion.

At this point he was certain that anything he did, thought, or said was "holy" because he was one with God. This conviction no doubt bolstered his self-confidence and led to the wildly unorthodox social and religious behavior that would become legendary.

John's first convert to "Perfectionism" seems to have been Harriet Holton, whom he married in 1838. As a team they developed John's complex beliefs and put them into practice at the commune he founded: The Putney Association of Perfectionists.

His flock grew. By 1843 his followers included twenty-eight adults and nine children with five hundred acres of land, seven houses, a print shop, and a store. Hard work and education were two of the commune's more mainstream values.

But something was happening behind the scenes and the

citizens of Putney were none too happy about it. The Perfectionists were practicing what John called Complex Marriage. It was complex because under this unusual doctrine every man was married to every woman. Monogamy was considered selfish and idolatrous. Sexual intercourse between consenting adults was fine as long as folks didn't get too attached to each other. Under John's system flirting and courting became unnecessary rituals of the primitive past. Sexual partners had only to gain each other's consent via the intervention of a third party, more often than not, Rev. Noyes himself.

It's easy to see how this worked out to John's advantage, it even neutralized "the curse," but how the good people of Putney reacted is another matter. The issue was this "consenting adults" business. John's pursuit of fifteen year old Lucinda J. Lamb began to undermine any credibility he may have established in town.

In 1847 Daniel Hall had nearly converted to Perfectionism, but apparently he experienced an attack of old-style conscience, pulling out at the last minute. He accused John of adultery. An arrest warrant was issued. Needless to say, the community sided with the accusers.

As historian William Hines recalled in 1911, "Mr. Noyes and his followers considered it prudent to remove to a place where they were sure of more liberal treatment."

Of course this meant New York. They settled in the town of Oneida, where John founded the now-famous Oneida Community.

They built the gigantic (93,000-square-foot) "Mansion House" where they all lived together, engaging in Complex Marriage and perfecting other unorthodox methods of social harmony.

Within Complex Marriage, the Perfectionists practiced a difficult form of birth control called *Male Continence*, a variety of coitus interruptus, i.e. "knowing when to quit." It required practice, especially among the community's younger, most testosterone-driven members. So a training program called *Ascending Fellowship* was developed in which the older, most godly members of the community would each select a fourteen year old virgin to spiritually guide and tutor. Men who mentored the young women were presumably already adept at Male Continence. The women who trained the boys were invariably beyond child-bearing age, and thus protected against the inevitable "accidents."

The convoluted nature of some of the resulting interpersonal relationships necessitated the process of *Mutual Criticism*, a precursor of today's group therapy. Community members took turns being reprimanded for breeches in social protocol, personal peculiarities, and spiritual flaccidity.

In *Without Sin*, his history of the Oneida Community, Spencer Klaw cites the criticism session of a Vermont native. The man was chastised for, "stiffness of character, too much gravity, and not enough veracity; an over-estimation of New England men and"—almost predictably—"too frequent mention of Vermont."

The Perfectionists also experimented with an early form of eugenics manipulation called *Stirpiculture*. Here the men and women who were deemed most physically, mentally, and spiritually ascended were given the responsibility of producing offspring. In his sixties at the time *Stirpiculture* was implemented, John Humphrey Noyes managed to sire nine of the fifty-eight children born during this experiment.

What some considered the most misguided of the Perfectionists' beliefs was the equality of the sexes. Rev. Noyes and his followers believed absolutely that men and women were completely equal, a notion still widely disputed.

As perverse as much of this may sound, Rev. Noyes's experiment was the most successful of the many nineteenth century utopian communities, flourishing for more than thirty years. In general its people were happy, well-educated, and the children produced by complex marriage were eager to remain at, or return to, the colony. As a visiting journalist wrote at the time, "I am bound to say as an honest reporter, that I looked in vain for the visible signs of either the suffering or the sin."

Alas, Oneida wasn't Utopia for everyone. Charles Guiteau dropped out in 1866 after failing to find any sexual partners. He condemned Perfectionism, saying it had been created solely to satisfy Mr. Noyes's sexual appetites. Premature sexual experience, he alleged, made the community women "small and thin and homely."

In 1881 Mr. Guiteau expanded his horizons. Having failed at theology, a law practice, bill collecting, and procreating at the Oneida Community, he took aim at politics by successfully assassinating James Abram Garfield, leaving the presidency of the United States to Vermonter Chester A. Arthur.

The Oneida Colony was destined to follow the pattern of many cults, before and since: when the charismatic leader steps down or dies, the community fails. Rev. Noyes's nineteenth century efforts at communal living, spiritual harmony, sexual equality, selective breeding, and improved conditions for workers evolved into a twentieth century business known the world over as Oneida Limited, producer of fine flatware.

The Mansion House still stands in Oneida NY and there are still houses in Putney, Vermont where the Perfectionists lived. No plaques mark them as historic destinations. Tourists can enter and leave town without ever knowing what began to take shape there.

ঌ THE MAN AND THE MOON ঵

Probably you have heard some weird things about the moon. That it is hollow. That it's an artificial structure. That there are military bases—maybe even extraterrestrial encampments—on the dark side that we can never see.

You can be sure most of these notions don't come from astronomers. In fact, it's difficult to determine just how they got started. The venerable "Old Man in the Moon" illusion has been around for a long time. The "Green Cheese" concept remains a puzzle to me. And the fact that "moon" rhymes with "June" has become an irritation. (Thankfully, the song "Moonlight in Vermont" avoids this cliché. In fact, none of the words rhyme.)

But I have to fess up, Vermont may well be partly guilty of moon myth making thanks to the work of one slightly eccentric Vermonter who left his mark in the skies above Bellows Falls during the late 19th century.

"Eccentric" might be the wrong word. In his day Seth Blake (August 21, 1817-June 25, 1904) was a well-liked and influential member of the community. Born in Brookfield, Seth learned the printer's trade in Montpelier. In 1839 he moved to Bellows Falls to work as a typesetter at the *Bellows Falls Gazette*. In 1844 Seth purchased the newspaper and expanded the business to include books and other printed material.

On August 16, 1842, he married Martha J. Glover of Concord, N. H. Together they had six sons and two daughters.

But even with solid professional standing and a good family,

Seth Blake remained ambitious, destined for bigger things.

Two of his brothers were practicing dentists in Connecticut. Seth apprenticed himself to one of them, Amos Shepard Blake. After mastering the profession, Seth came home to Bellows Falls and hung out his shingle. It read:

DR. S. M. BLAKE, OPERATIONS ON TEETH.

Apparently he also crafted top quality, artful, porcelain false teeth, which were high-tech at the time.

His solid professional stature allowed him to influence local and even statewide events. For example, he was instrumental in bringing four railroads to town, which contributed tremendously to the area's prosperity.

Dr. Blake was widely known as a writer and lecturer. During the Civil War he argued persuasively and tirelessly for the preservation of the union.

Beyond seeing to the wellbeing of teeth, town, state, and nation, Dr. Blake had some fascinating private interests. It is claimed he was the first to discover the true age of the great pyramid of Cheops. He invented what may have been the first combination lock for safes. And Dr. Blake had excellent eyesight. He was considered to be the best marksman with a rifle in this part of New England; he was known as a "crack shot."

The latter may relate to his greatest interest—astronomy.

Back in 1837 the youthful Seth Blake had observed large spots on the sun. The phenomenon piqued his curiosity, giving birth to a life-long avocation.

Even as a lad of twenty he had some knowledge of optics, so he built his own telescope. Later, when he was more prosperous, he purchased a 76 inch telescope for $225. It was bigger than and superior to most telescopes in the state. He had it mounted in a revolving observatory on top of his house at 75 Atkinson Street.

From there the dentist moonlighting as an astronomer made his first great discovery: a new star. Or rather an old star, one that appeared only intermittently.

Here's an account from the *St. Paul Daily Globe*, September 22, 1885:

"Apropos to the new star which has made its appearance, astronomical records show that in the year 940 a bright star appeared and in course of time was lost to sight. Again in 1204 and in 1571 what was supposed to be the same star came within ken. Last winter [Dr.] S. M. Blake of Bellows Falls, Vt. happened to note that 314 years having passed since it last appeared; he supposed that it might be due again about this time. So during the last few months he swept the sky with his glass, and on the 27th of August discovered the newcomer in Andromeda. He foretells that in the next twelve months it will grow so bright as to rival Jupiter and then it will disappear. It will probably not be seen again until more than three hundred years have again rolled away."

But here's the thing: Dr. Blake was convinced he had identified the Star of Bethlehem, the same star that the Three Magi followed to where it cast its light upon the manger in which Jesus was born.

Gary Nowak, former president of the Vermont Astronomical Society, tells me that what Dr. Blake actually saw was the Supernova in M31 "the Andromeda Galaxy." Of course Dr. Blake couldn't know what a Supernova was. As Gary explains it, "The supernova is like a giant firecracker going off. Once the firecracker explodes with a brilliant flash, that's it, and there is not much left of anything. Certainly the scattered gas and dust particles from the supernova explosion will not light up again."

And, though he got a lot of press at the time, Dr. Blake was not the first to discover it. "First discovery" was credited to E. Hartwig for his August 20, 1885 observation.

But the irrepressible Dr. Blake kept watching the skies, and soon he was to make a most startling discovery. And this time it would be his and his alone.

He first announced it in *The Bellow Falls Times* on December 15, 1887. And what an announcement it was!

Okay. Now before we go on, remember that Seth Blake

computed the age of the great pyramid. Discovered a supernova. And, perhaps most important, he had extraordinarily good eyesight. So, he announced. . .

A NEW DISCOVERY
The Moon has Been Inhabited

Dr. Blake starts by saying that published pictures of the moon, specifically those that ran in the March 1885 issue of *Century Magazine,* are inaccurate. He doesn't go so far as to say any photographs have been doctored, but he does assert that he was able to see something no one else had discovered—gigantic structures on the moon. Perhaps the remains of a whole lunar civilization.

"For nearly forty years, with the aid of a telescope," Seth writes, "[I have] made the study of the moon a kind of specialty, hoping all the while to find some evidence that our satellite has, at some period of the past, been the abode of life and intelligence."

Apparently he got exactly what he had hoped for.

Dr. Blake admitted that it required courage to speak out when other scientists had heralded the impossibility of lunar life, but he went on to reveal what he saw, and gave precise coordinates so that others can see it, too.

Between the crater Archimedes and the Apennine Mountains he discovered "a vast wall of more than two hundred miles in extent. . ."

At its top the wall forms a 90 degree angle and extends to the left, in a perfectly straight line, some thirty miles.

"This wall," he wrote, "is arranged in sections, and each section is of the same height, length, and thickness."

He described the top of these sections as being "oval or domed-shape, and . . . appear as if covered over with some kind of silicious or glossy substance."

Glossy? Why should that be?"

"To utilize our earth-shine in lighting up the darkness of their long and dreary nights. Behold the great mirrors that send

forth their beams of light across their continents and what was
once their seas!"

Close to this wall he discerned "a great ship canal," two hundred miles long, six miles wide, and several feet deep, "cut as
straight as a line could be drawn, and whose bottom is as smooth
as if paved with granite blocks."

He attributed all this oversized construction work to "a race
of men far superior in physical power to any type of human family that have peopled this earth since history, or even tradition,
began."

And—you might ask—why was Dr. Seth Blake of Bellows
Falls, Vermont the only scientist or astronomer to discover these
massive ruins on the moon?

Well, essentially, says Dr. Blake, because no one else was
looking for them. "Their great magnitude being so much out of
proportion to anything looked for as a work of human accom-
plishment is probably the reason why they have not been recognized before."

In short, Dr. Blake believed he had discovered irrefutable
proof that the moon had once been inhabited. That the inhabitants—no doubt larger, stronger, and more advanced than mere
earthlings—had for some reason vanished. And the remains of
their once thriving civilization had been overlooked for centuries
simply because no one expected it to be there.

Well, maybe.

Dr. Blake was so certain of his discoveries that he would not
even entertain the arguments of skeptics. He challenged them to
look and see for themselves. "See all this," he said, "and then tell
us who can, that the moon was never inhabited."

Dr. Blake had no explanation for why the moon civilization
ended and what caused the water and atmosphere to disappear.
He couldn't even judge when the tragedy occurred.

But the stubborn dentist, who lived to be 88 years old, never
withdrew his theory of giant moon men, colossal constructions,
and a vast system of canals.

As with his Star of Bethlehem discovery, Dr. Blake received

little to no support from the scientific community.

Possibly, since he first announced his discovery, the moon monuments have continued their disintegration into dust, for they are not visible to any modern telescopes nor were they discovered by our Apollo Astronauts.

Perhaps the final act of this science fiction drama came in 1969 when Dr. Blake's telescope was in the possession of his grandson, Harry Blake, of Claremont, New Hampshire. Mr. Blake invited members of the Bellows Falls Historical Society to his home to watch mankind's first lunar journey: the Apollo 11 Astronauts on their way to the moon.

How surprising it would have been if the lunar explorers had reached the moon only to observe another structure described by Dr. Blake: ". . . a figure suggesting the letter B with the lower end of the letter unfinished!"

A giant "B"? Perhaps standing for. . . Blake?

✑ SHOOTING THE BULL ∾

Anyone who's explored ancient ruins—castles, forts, deserted mansions—has enjoyed the thrill of then and now colliding. But modern ruins are another thing: there is something unsettling about them.

When Dr. Gerald Bull's Space Research Corporation was abandoned around 1990, it was a brand new facility. Straddling the US-Canada border in the town of Jay, Vermont, this mysterious private compound was state-of-the-art, science fiction-like, resembling something from a James Bond thriller. Today it looks like the aftermath of an atomic blast.

So what happened up there in the Vermont wilds?

The story of Dr. Gerald Bull and his Space Research Corporation seems almost forgotten, but with American troops still in Iraq and Afghanistan, and the international tension that results, perhaps this fascinating story is worth another look.

Many specialists considered Dr. Bull the most brilliant artillery scientist of the 20th century. Born in North Bay, Ontario in 1928, his lonely childhood led him to the works of Jules Verne. The big cannon in From the Earth to the Moon (1875) must have become the compass for his life. His ambition was to construct a gigantic gun capable of firing projectiles from the earth's surface into outer space.

As a student, he was gifted and motivated. At 24 he earned a Ph.D. in aeronautical engineering. By age 31 he was head of the Aerophysics Department of the Canadian Armament and Research Development Establishment (CARDE). Along the way he married, had seven children, but never served in the military nor owned a firearm. In fact, he was not especially militaristic. His agenda was simple: cannons are better than rockets.

In 1961, Washington began to take an interest in Dr. Bull's work with high altitude ballistics, oversized guns, and the manufacture of long range shells for use in Vietnam. But he was Canadian, so there was trouble with certain U.S. security clearances. With Senator Barry Goldwater as his sponsor, Dr. Bull was made an instant American by a rare Senatorial fiat used only twice before.

But Dr. Bull's dealings with the U.S. soured as the powers-that-be turned their attention from cannons to rockets. He, however, never wavered in his love of guns. Big guns. Cannons of unheard of dimensions. He was convinced he could fire bullets the size of propane tanks into orbit. Possibly he could start his own alternative space program based on cannons instead of rockets.

After the Americans abandoned him, Dr. Bull continued to develop, test, manufacture, and sell his extended-range weaponry from his remote compound in the northern Vermont-Quebec wilderness. Privacy was essential as was the company's strategic position on the border. Because arms-export laws were different in the two countries, the materials he needed, and the weapons he manufactured, could be shipped to or from either nation.

On site he had his own artillery range, telemetry towers, launch-control buildings, radar tracking station, workshops, and machine shops. He employed more than three hundred people.

Over the years Dr. Bull attempted to sell his space-cannon design to NATO, the Pentagon, Canada, China, Israel, and finally, to Iraq. That's when real trouble started. He agreed to make the Iraqis a cannon that could put dozens, perhaps hundreds, of satellites into orbit. The Iraqis could become a genuine space power—the only Arab space power—for as little as $5,000.00 a pop.

Of course Saddam Hussein assured Dr. Bull that his super-gun would be used only for communications and surveillance; it would never have a combat application.

This Iraqi super-launcher would have a barrel five hundred feet long, weigh 2,100 tons, and fire projectiles the size of telephone booths.

While Saddam Hussein was delighted with the prospect, the Israelis were not at all pleased. Such a cannon—unwieldy as it may be—could be used to dump a load of nerve gas or a nuclear bomb onto any capital in the world.

Time for preemptive measures.

On March 22, 1990, while in Brussels, Dr. Bull was greeted at his hotel room by person or persons unknown.

Ironic, isn't it, that the designer of the biggest gun in the world was felled by one of the smallest: a silenced 7.65 millimeter automatic pistol. Dr. Bull took five slugs to the back of the head.

In 1991 Israeli secret service agents admitted to the assassination.

ॐ ॐ

I visited the compound recently with my friend Jim Defilippi. We found it an eerie experience. We felt like archeologists entering a war zone when we saw the flattened guard house. It looked like a glacier had rolled over it.

After a considerable climb we found buildings, graffiti stained and weather damaged. Signs of vandalism were everywhere.

We were surprised at how much the forest had reclaimed in so few years. Jim and I poked around, wondering what the wild undergrowth might conceal. Were there locked doorways leading to underground passageways? Might secret documents be stashed among the litter of overturned file cabinets? Were there mementoes—a lighter, keychain, or ballpoint pen—once belonging to Dr. Bull?

Of course we really wanted to see a cannon, a supergun, maybe the prototype for the monster Dr. Bull had promised to Saddam Hussein. Could such a weapon be lurking somewhere in the tall grass like a giant anaconda?

We'd heard that one remained on the compound's Canadian side, but, given the political situation—homeland security and all—we were hesitant to cross into Canada, especially from here.

At length our inspection revealed an eerie, isolated ruin, but—and this may sound familiar—there were no weapons of mass destruction.

THE NEW ENGLAND FAT MEN'S CLUB
Girth & Mirth in the Green Mountains

It could never happen today. Healthier-than-thou attitudes or political correctness would snuff it out before the first bite. But in 1903 we lived in different world.

The tiny village of Wells River, in the town of Newbury, Vermont, was a thriving place where railroads and commerce kept shops hopping and guest houses full.

At some point that November, Jerome Hale, the congenial owner of Hale's Tavern, stopped to observe the ten traveling salesmen clustered around his fireplace. They seemed to be having a wonderful time. And they all were conspicuously obese. He then enjoyed a moment of inspiration: Why not form an alliance? When he posed the idea to his portly patrons, they loved it: The New England Fat Men's Club was born.

Everyone enthusiastically agreed to recruit new members and to attend biannual meetings—one at Hale's Tavern, the other at some more exotic location, like Concord, New Hampshire, Portland, Maine, or Revere Beach in Massachusetts.

Membership requirements were simple: you had to weigh at least 200 pounds. The initiation fee was just one dollar; there were no annual dues.

Not surprisingly, many people were eager to join a club that encouraged its members to make the most of themselves. By the fall 1904 meeting, this novel fraternal order—founded on good fellowship and dedicated to the proposition that fat people are happy people—had attracted 110 qualified members. It was no surprise that membership kept expanding. By 1910, enrollment had reached 3,000. Fifteen years later, New England could no longer contain the Fat Men's Club. There were over 10,000 members, representing 38 states and eight foreign countries.

A typical meeting began on Saturday with the ceremonial weigh-in. This aspect of participation could be tricky. Judge Hammond Baldwin of Wells River routinely began gorging himself the moment a gathering was announced. Frank Sibley's go-to-meeting attire included two horse hitching weights hung on his suspenders. For most, however, the qualifications were effortlessly met, though some members were more qualified than others. Frank X. Gignac of Franklin Falls, New Hampshire, weighed an enviable 400 pounds. Portland Maine's Arthur Moulton carried the most weight, tipping the scales at 435 pounds. Later, with the encouragement of his peers, Mr. Moulton attained a magnificent 473 pounds.

After giving the Fairbanks scales a grueling workout, the men assembled on the tavern lawn for an afternoon of sporting events. Cigar-chomping David Wilkie (222-265 lbs), the club's first president, won the 100-yard dash, but he only had one opponent. By the time the racers were able to slow down, it had become a two-hundred yard dash. They had to cancel the tug-of-war because the rope broke, causing the men to tumble. The following year they replaced the rope with a chain. Competitors quickly discovered they could tug just as well sitting down.

Mr. Hale himself won the potato race, though his competitors groused that he had an unfair advantage. At a mere 207 pounds, he was the only player who could see the potato when it was between his feet.

When it came to baseball, a team could win in two ways: by total score or by total poundage. In 1905 Mr. Gignac's winning team prevailed at both, with fifteen runs and 2,279 pounds. Mr. Moulton's team weighed a measly 2,143 pounds, but the winners had invented ingenious ways of streamlining the game, like taking shortcuts from first to third base.

Some people suggested a pole vaulting competition, but the idea was scrapped out of concern for the poles. As always, Mr. B.

M. Wentworth (246 lbs.) of Somerville, Massachusetts, won his favorite athletic event, the pie-eating contest. Oddly, he was also a champion high-kicker who set the club's record of 7'3," even after polishing off his pie. He was believed to have a wooden leg, which may explain one triumph if not the other.

A 7:00 pm business meeting followed the afternoon games. Officers were elected, including one president with six vice presidents, one for each New England state. Pounds, rather than ballots often decided the outcome. The gathering's main function, however, was to alert everyone that dinner was just an hour away.

Tavern-keeper Hale routinely outdid himself with lavish banquets. He had each table modified with concave cutouts to accommodate the sitters' contours. The highly caloric nine-course feed virtually guaranteed each man would find the experience broadening. Speakers, a live orchestra, along with other entertainment filled the remaining time, but nothing was ever permitted to impede the non-stop hilarity.

As club president, Mr. Wilkie decreed, "We're fat and we're making the most of it." The press loved the organization, covering it in great detail. They also contributed many well-rounded members to its roster.

Out-of-town meetings were organized partly for the purpose of recruitment. The group's 1910 gala, for example, was at the Revere House in Boston. Of the 250 present, 20 weighed in at over 300 pounds. Local electric trolleys blew at least five fuses toting the revelers around the city. During an outing at Revere Beach, the roller coaster faired no better. Of the 75 who boarded, most required two seats.

Their antics on the beach proved vastly entertaining to onlookers. Group prestige swelled as the grinning 305-pound President William Quimby was repeatedly mistaken for Teddy Roosevelt, a notion he was slow to set straight.

Members went to inflated lengths to attend meetings. Samuel Chesley Drew of York Beach, Maine, persuaded a train to make an unscheduled stop by insisting that "a large party wanted to board." When the train arrived, the 430 pound Mr.

Drew waddled on. Having arrived at his hotel, he got stuck in the taxi. Later, his chair collapsed under him.

Sadly, the New England Fat Men's Club was also destined to collapse. The world changed. Membership dwindled. Fewer than forty members attended the twentieth anniversary meeting. Of them, only three were founding members. With so few participants, they couldn't afford a live orchestra; they had to settle for "canned" music.

In 1927, the year Jerome Hale died, the New England Fat Men's Club died, too. Twenty-nine years later, Hale's Tavern, the club's headquarters, was demolished to be replaced by a Gulf station. Still, the organization had a pretty good run, active from 1903 to 1927. It was unique, the only such affiliation in the U.S. As far as I can determine, it was the only one in the world.

With its special handshakes, badges, cigar-snipping watch fobs, secret passwords, not to mention the zeppelin-like red, white, and blue umbrellas, the Fat Men's Club lampooned the exclusive and secretive fraternal orders proliferating at the time: the Masons, Odd Fellows, Moose, B.P.O.E. etc. With its unfailing good humor the club helped ease us through World War I while trying to teach us not to take ourselves too seriously.

These days there is no place for an anti-fitness club, no place for jokes at the expense of overweight people, and little tolerance for same-sex societies. Today, few 200-pound men would be viewed as obese.

The club's philosophy might be best expressed in its toast, which is perhaps the way it should be remembered:

A toast to us my good, kind friends
To bless the things we eat,
For it has been full many a year
Since we have seen our feet.
But who would lose a precious pound
By trading sweets for sours?
It takes a mighty girth indeed
To hold such hearts as ours.

❧ SECTION IV. ❧
IT CAN'T HAPPEN HERE!

I have borrowed Sinclair Lewis's title, and his irony, for this section dealing with "out of place events." By that I mean historical occurrences that, for one reason or another, seem to have happened in the wrong place—that wrong place being Vermont. While none of the events may be especially weird in themselves, they are unusual simply because one would never guess such things could go on right here in our state.

It just can't happen here.

Or so we might think.

❧ "WHAT GENTLEMEN WERE THOSE?" ❧

Many Vermonters venture south to explore Civil War Battlegrounds—but they don't need to. As it turns out, the northernmost engagement of the war between the states took place right here in the Green Mountains. What's more, the Vermont town of St. Albans was actually claimed for the Confederacy.

The so-called "St. Albans Raid" was a daring act of war played out with all the secrecy and precision of a modern terrorist attack.

Beginning around October 10, 1864, twenty-two young strangers began to appear on the streets of St. Albans. They arrived in twos and threes, disguised as horse traders, tourists, preachers, even invalids. They attracted no more attention than any of the thousands of travelers who passed through this busy railroad town. All of them seemed friendly, polite, and they mixed well with the citizens. Each made frequent purchases from the stores, patronized the hotels, and dined at the restaurants. They were always eager to chat, showing a flattering interest in the habits of St. Albans's 4,000 citizens.

But of course their interest hid sinister intent. When they talked about local game and tried to borrow guns for hunting, they were actually assessing to what extent the locals were armed. When one of them brazenly called at Governor Smith's mansion to admire the grounds and stable, he was really preparing to steal horses for a getaway.

Their leader, the mastermind of the raid, was a twenty-one year old southern aristocrat named Lt. Bennett H. Young who, along with his men, had recently escaped from northern prisons and had sought asylum in Canada.

Lt. Young had three motives for the terror that was to come: First, he hoped to help replenish the Confederacy's dwindling coffers. Second, he reasoned that if he were to assault the largest Northern town closest to neutral Canada, Union armies would be dispatched north, taking pressure off the weakening South. And third and most frightening, he wanted to give the Yankees a taste of the horror and devastation Gen. Sheridan had inflicted in the Shenandoah Valley.

≈≫

Wednesday, October 19, 1864—the day after market day—was particularly quiet in St. Albans. Rainy weather kept people off the streets. Hundreds of men were at work in machine shops and railroad depot buildings. Forty town leaders were away, doing business in Montpelier and Burlington. It was an ideal day to attack.

Nervous commandos mingled with unsuspecting townspeople, watching the town clock, waiting for it to strike 3:00. The moment the bell sounded the onslaught began. A uniformed Lt. Young rode up and down the street with a revolver in each hand. Between rebel yells he declared, "I take possession of this town in the name of the Confederate States of America."

In precisely coordinated maneuvers three clusters of raiders simultaneously descended on the town's three banks.

Four entered the St. Albans Bank, seized employees by their throats and threatened them with navy revolvers. "Not a word," one said, "we're Confederate soldiers come to take your town. We shall have all your money. If you resist, we'll blow your brains out." This action took 12 minutes.

At exactly the same time five more rebels hit the Franklin County Bank. "We are Confederate soldiers. There are a hundred of us. We've come to rob your banks and burn your town." In fewer than 15 minutes the robbery was over.

Meanwhile, another band of four plundered the First National Bank. "If you offer any resistance I will shoot you dead."

While the banks were being robbed, armed conspirators outside were herding terrified citizens onto the village green. Though the situation seemed right for a mass execution, the raiders were actually trying to contain information about the raid.

Synchronously, Rebels who'd stolen horses prepared them for flight. Still others created mayhem with Rebel yells, gun shots, and incendiary bombs. Luckily, bad aims and rainy weather kept the fires from doing any significant damage.

In roughly twenty minutes it was over. Twenty-two young confederate soldiers held the town of St. Albans hostage.

In spite of the threats, commotion, and terror, several townspeople performed acts of heroism. Few were hurt. Three who resisted were shot, though only one died of his wounds. He was the only casualty. One of the raiders was hit by a bullet as they escaped with 208,000 stolen dollars and bonds. He survived.

Although the Vermonters wasted no time in organizing a pursuit, the Rebels made it to the safety of Canada—where 13 of them were arrested and $80,000 confiscated.

Their trial was long, costly, and ultimately unsatisfying. The Canadian justice system decided they had no jurisdiction in the matter. And—because the raid was an act of war—the laws that would permit extradition did not apply. The Rebels were released; the stolen money was returned to them.

In time the raiders made their way back home to the Blue Grass region of Kentucky where they assumed important roles in their communities. Their leader, Lt. Bennett Young—now Colonel Young—became a prominent lawyer, author, and railroad executive.

Forty seven years after the raid, when things had cooled down, Col. Young met with some of St. Albans's town fathers at the Ritz-Carlton in Montreal. One of the Vermonters, John Branch, who had witnesses the raid when he was a boy, described Young as "...a typical southern gentleman, as loyal to his re-united country as he was to his cherished Confederacy."

Col. Young recalled "the Vairmont Yankee scare party" as a reckless escapade of flaming youth and he wondered that he ever undertook it.

The Colonel died in 1919 at age 76, a respected citizen, and, in the southern United States, a hero. Perhaps some Vermonters see him a hero too. Not so much for commanding this audacious Civil War engagement, but for the heroic blunders that he made.

For example, at the various banks the Rebels overlooked thousands of dollars, large sums in bonds, and bags of precious gold. They deliberately left behind several sacks of silver because they were too heavy to carry. In his history of the raid L.L. Dutcher says, "It seems that they actually left behind more money than they took...."

One especially significant tactical blunder is that Col. Young failed to silence the telegraph office. As a result, help was on the way before the twenty minute raid was complete.

Although the Rebels fired dozens—maybe hundreds—of shots, many directed at townspeople, their aim seemed consistently bad.

As terrifying as the raid must have been, it was not without its comic elements. During the robbery of the First National Bank a retired soldier named General John Nason was seated in a corner reading a newspaper. Gen. Nason was about 90 years old and extremely deaf. He was so absorbed in his newspaper that he missed the robbery altogether. Then, when two of the raiders subdued an incoming customer, the General tottered over to the struggling men to remind them that "two upon one is not fair play."

Then, after the rebels had made off with their loot, General Nason approached one of the terrified bankers and mildly inquired, "What gentlemen were those?"

To answer his question, they were: Bennett H. Young, Squire Turner Teavis, William T. Teavis, Alamanda Pope Bruce, Samuel Eugene Lacky, Marcus Spurr, Charles Moore Swager, George Scott, Cabel Wallace, James Alexander Dotty, Joseph McGorth, Samuel Simpson Gregg, Dudley Moore, Thomas Bronson

Collins, William H. Hutcherson, John McInnis, Charles Higbie, Lewis Price, Daniel Butterworth, John E. Moss, someone identified as Rev. Cameron and a Mr. Saunders.

Most were between 20 and 26 years old except Mr. McGorth, who was 38.

Contrary to the opinion at the time, they were not low-life hoodlums, but well-educated, upper class young men, typical Southern gentlemen from good, in some cases aristocratic families. Bennett Young himself was a staunch Presbyterian who hated liquor, profanity, and tobacco. Mr. Wallace was the nephew of Kentucky Senator John Crittenden. Another raider's uncle was former Vice President Breckinridge.

In hindsight it is difficult to determine whether we owe it to the rebels' ineptitude or their restraint, but the St. Albans Raid had the potential to have been the state's worst tragedy. Instead we remember it as one of the most dramatic, fascinating and colorful episodes in Vermont history.

❧ THE INVISIBLE EMPIRE ❧

After the Civil War an insidious contagion slowly worked its way from the old south into the Green Mountains of Vermont.

My first inkling that it was here came in the 1970s when a friend, working in his Bristol barn, made an odd discovery. He found a secret closet containing white cloth robes and boxes of printed material.

Devil worship? No, not exactly. What he had discovered was that a previous owner of his property had been a member of the infamous Ku Klux Klan.

But here in Vermont?

Although some people might not realize it—I certainly didn't—there was once an active chapter of the Klan here, with thousands of members all over the state. As recently as 1927 white-klad klanspersons (the membership included men and women) marched proudly beside their heavily flowered floats in Montpelier's Fourth of July parade.

In spite of its pro-American, God, Country, and Family Values rhetoric, the Klan of the 1920s wasn't so much an attempt to promote ideas and ideals as it was a subversive movement that eroded societal harmony, disguising its venom in the uniform of super-patriotism.

Its two principal targets—Blacks and Jews—were not present here in sufficient quantity to keep the Klanspersons occupied, so "The Hidden Empire" had to focus its hatred on two other conspicuous populations: Catholics and French Canadians.

106

Needless to say, Vermont's klan didn't originate spontaneously among the Green Mountains. It was the product of an aggressive recruitment campaign, controlled out of the Northern New England klan headquarters in Rochester, New Hampshire. Efforts began in earnest in 1922 when visiting KKK organizers canvassed the state. At that time they discovered that certain cadets at Norwich University were already members.

In 1924 full-time organizers were assigned to Vermont. They relocated here to begin a concentrated campaign of klan building. By the end of the year the KKK had a solid foothold. The "Corporation Department" of the Secretary of State's office received applications from the Knights of the Ku Klux Klan and the Women of the Ku Klux Klan to do business in Vermont. Secretary Aaron H. Grout declined, saying the applications failed to state, "the business to be done." Also, they "do not state anything to be done in Vermont which is within the meaning of the word 'business' as used in the foreign [i.e. non-Vermont] corporation law."

But everyone knew what business the klan was in.

Invitation-only meetings were held all over the state, including Springfield, Barre, Windsor, Bellows Falls, Rutland, and Burlington. At first they were gentle coaxing sessions conducted in semi-secret, but without the intimidating high-ceremony and white robes. Later outdoor rallies were staged in full costume and with much pomp and circumstance. Bands played and crosses burned. Over 2,000 people attended a September 1, 1924 meeting in St. Johnsbury.

On May 2, 1925, five thousand men and women held the first public open air "konclave" at the Lamoille Country fairgrounds in Morrisville. Total membership in Vermont at that time exceeded 14,000 people.

The deceiving part of much of this is that the rallies and recruitment were done in a holiday atmosphere of fun and good fellowship. The social, good-neighborly aspects of Klannishness were emphasized while its roots of hatred and terrorism remained subsurface. This was evident in the "if-you-join-I'll-join" attitude of many Vermonters and in the photographs of Vermont rallies that show, even while in full regalia, that facemasks were not used.

As Maudean Neill states in her fascinating book about Klan activity in Vermont (*Fiery Crosses in the Green Mountains*, 1989), "The unlawful acts were undoubtedly planned and performed by the minority. It was this minority of planners or 'organizers' followed by the unsuspecting crowd which became a problem equal to any this country already possessed, turning citizen against citizen."

For example, after a Barre couple entertained a Jewish house guest, they were anonymously accused of "harboring Jews." A bootlegger was brought to justice with the help of a klansman. And a Highgate merchant received a menacing reprimand for "courting a married woman." At one point seven crosses were burning at the same time in the especially sinful city of Montpelier. Another burned on Burlington's breakwater.

When the *Windsor Vermont Journal* opposed the klan, calling them "Klu Klux Klowns," the editor received a letter saying "Unless certain newspaper reporters in the north stop attacking the klan, they will be taught the same lesson that some editors in the south have learned."

Yet the klan continued its attacks, now focusing on Vermont's Roman Catholic population.

Klan members somehow got it into their heads that vast supplies of arms and ammunition were stored in secret arsenals in the basements of Catholic Churches, ready to be used at some future time. When the Pope gave the word, Catholics would lead an armed uprising, seizing the government and subjugating all Protestants.

In Burlington assistant kleagle William Moyers, after downing a bit too much illegal whiskey, tried to convince provisional Klansmen William McCready and Gordon F. Wells, "that there were enough guns, ammunition, acid, gas, airplanes and war material concealed beneath St. Mary's Cathedral of the Immaculate Conception* to blow up the New England states and all the Protestants in them."

What's more, he said he had personally seen this vast

underground armory. He told of a mysterious "third cellar" way below the church which he himself had explored. He'd been discovered there, he boasted, and had to shoot his way out.

Apparently it was more of an incredulous "show me" attitude than any real wish to inflict damage that inspired McCready and Wells to follow Moyers into the church. But, he warned them, they might have to shoot their way out. So the men stopped at Wood's Sporting Goods Store and bought revolvers for the occasion. They then drove to South Champlain Street where they parked behind Cathedral High School. From there they walked to the church.

Moyers entered through an unlocked window under the chapel. He was on his way to unlock the door and let his companions in, but became distracted by objects in the vestry. He helped himself to some vestments, candles, a crucifix, and other church property, the total value of which was $164.40.

From outside Father Joseph Gillis saw the flickering flashlight within the church and called the police. After some scrambling, and a brief exchange of gunfire, the klansmen were finally apprehended.

This sacrilegious act and the subsequent cover-up were considered by many to be one of the most sensational outrages in Burlington criminal history.

After the trial, the klan's reputation in Vermont plummeted; its demise quickly followed. People saw how stupid the whole thing was. What the events did, I suspect, was convince many tolerant Vermonters that these Ku Klux Klowns were really serious about hate.

All in all, the KKK's run in Vermont lasted for only about four years. It was ancient history long before the national klan disbanded in 1944.

*(St. Mary's Cathedral was formerly at the corner of Cherry and St. Paul Streets. It fell to arson in March, 1972. The event was not klan-related.)

↝ LOWLY VERMONTERS ↜

The hatred that fueled the Ku Klux Klan also manifested with apparent innocence in another sordid undertaking we Vermonters prefer to dismiss from our memories.

Back in the nineteen twenties and thirties, 138 Church Street in Burlington was the office of the Eugenics Survey of Vermont, directed by Henry Farnham Perkins, a native Vermonter whose roots went back to the Mayflower.

Dr. Perkins was a Zoology professor at the University of Vermont. In his office, within an unobtrusive filing cabinet, were accumulating data about the state's "undesirables": the drunks, the "feeble-minded," the paupers, the prostitutes, the mental and physical "defectives." Dr. Perkins was putting together human "pedigree charts" to be used in population engineering and control.

According to historian Kevin Dann's sobering article "The Purification of Vermont" (*Vermont Affairs*, Summer/Fall 1987), "The 'science' of eugenics was a precursor of modern racism—its proponents believed in the existence of racial stereotypes, accepted the myth that certain races (particularly that of northern Europe) possessed a monopoly of desired characteristics, and thought that racial differences were invariably caused by heredity and thus were resistant to modification."

Miss Harriet E. Abbott was the first field worker employed by the Vermont Eugenics Survey. Marion Wadman was hired next. The women's routine was to drive around the back roads of rural

110

communities, visiting people, feigning interest, acquiring family histories. They were chatty and pleasant. They wrote polite "thank you" notes. And they filed the data. More often than not their "targets" had no idea what they were being targeted for.

Using the acquired information, charts were drawn up and used to identify where the "bad seed" in a family began, and how it spread. "By the end of 1925," Kevin Dann writes, "the Survey had pedigree charts for 62 families, including some 4,642 people. Of these 766 were paupers, 380 were 'feeble-minded,' 119 had prison records. There were 73 illegitimate children, 202 sex offenders, and 75 with physical defects such as blindness or paralysis."

Dr. Perkins questioned the accuracy of these figures, maintaining they were "Unquestionably much too low...."

To Vermont's most powerful and influential, Dr. Perkins's data "scientifically" supported what they already knew: that French-Canadian and Irish immigration, coupled with the emigration of Vermont's youth, were ruining the state.

All this eventually led to Act 174 of Vermont law, passed by the Vermont legislature on March 31, 1931, which stated, "Henceforth it shall be the policy of the state to prevent procreation of idiots, imbeciles, feeble-minded or insane persons, when the public welfare, and the welfare of idiots, imbeciles, feeble-minded or insane persons likely to procreate, can be improved by voluntary sterilization as herein provided."

Of myriad innocent Vermonters affected by the eugenics movement, the Abenaki were hit hardest. Many went into hiding, left, or took on French Canadian names. Some estimates hold that nearly 300 Abenaki people were sterilized, not always voluntarily. Some were institutionalized.

Interestingly, Vermont's sterilization law was almost identical to a law passed in Hitler's Germany two years later. Ours was very specific in its intent. It aimed at relieving the state of "the social and economic drag of avoidable low-grade Vermonters," according to Henry Perkins's report, issued in 1931 and sent to every Vermont library and leader.

That law wasn't repealed until 1967, long after similar ideas were opposed by force in Germany during World War II.

Admittedly the Eugenics Survey of Vermont, like the Klan, was part of a national effort. It didn't arise from, nor was it limited to, Vermont alone.

But the point is, it can happen here, and it did, even though it seems completely out of place and totally inconsistent with Vermont's attitudes about tolerance, equality and the sanctity of human rights.

NOTE: For more on this unpleasant subject, see *Breeding Better Vermonters: the Eugenics Project in the Green Mountain State* by Nancy L Gallagher (1999. University Press of New England)

～ MYSTERIES
OF THE MORMON MONUMENT ✎

Perhaps it is best to end this section of Vermont's unpleasant memories on a more cheerful note. To do so, let's journey to the southern Vermont town of Whitingham.

There a simple granite marker atop Stimpson Hill has a remarkable history. Its apparent purpose is to commemorate the site where Mormon leader Brigham Young was born. But the monument, like Mormonism itself, has always been shrouded in mystery.

The first mystery is that it just seemed appear, magically, as did the stone tablets of Moses. The story is that more than 100 years ago property owner Gerald Wheeler invited his wife Ethel out for a buggy ride. He hitched up the horses and off they went.

When they returned home sometime later, there it was: the Brigham Young Monument.

Was this a miracle? A coincidence? It certainly was a mystery. How could it just appear like that?

The second mystery is its meaning. Is it exactly what it seems, a commemorative marker honoring the site where the Mormon Leader was born? Or is it something else, a subtle form of social protest, a gentle criticism of Mormonism and their advocacy of such practices as polygamy?

Interpretation of the inscription seems to rest on a single word: "equipment." Does it have some archaic meaning that escapes today's readers? Might it refer, for example, to Mr. Young's farm machinery?

To be sure, the Mormons themselves were never too fond of the marker or its ambiguity. Which led to the third and most recent mystery.

On Friday, July 30, 1999, Donny Brown, occupant of the nearby cabin, was mowing his lawn. He stopped short and gasped, "My God, it's gone!"

Staring at a gaping hole in the ground, he realized the Mormon Monument had vanished!

Another miracle? Probably not. The ragged cavity suggested the memorial—and its cement base—had been ripped from the earth as if by a tractor and chain.

Mr. Brown reported the disappearance to town authorities and to the local historical society. Constable Richard Williams determined that the monument had been "unlawfully removed"—in other words, stolen.

The Whitingham Historical Society quickly issued a "Missing Monument" bulletin. It depicted the purloined plaque and questioned, "...how a Whitingham historical monument could just... disappear...?"

Good question.

The first clue came when investigators reexamined the hole. Beside it they discovered what was, in effect, a new monument, an anodized post bearing a Plexiglas plaque. Its verbose inscription concluded with the words, "placed [here] by the Church of Latter Day Saints," i.e. the Mormons.

A pretty good clue, but only circumstantial evidence of theft. Nonetheless, it caused suspicion to fall directly on the Mormons themselves.

A handful of residents recalled that less than a week before, hundreds of Mormons had gathered in town to celebrate their "Pioneer Day." And certain Mormons, it was well known, had long taken offense at the original stone monument and its ambiguous message.

Anyway, after making sure property owner Ray Purinton had not given anyone permission to remove the inscribed stone, Historical Society investigator Betsy McKinley took the next logical step—she phoned the Mormon Church in Sharon, Vermont.

There she spoke with employee Joe Mender and asked him straight out, "Did you take our stone?"

Naturally, being a good Mormon, he was unable to lie. "Yes," he said, "I did." Then the culprit assured Ms. McKinley the stone had not been destroyed . . . yet.

But when asked to return it, the thief hesitated. He said he'd have to check with Headquarters in Salt Lake City, suggesting a conspiracy much more far-reaching than Vermont itself.

At Mormon central, Ray Bryant of the "historic facilities division" dodged the question, deferring it to a vacationing official who wouldn't return for another week.

He also insisted the stone *had not* been *stolen.* But the fact is, it had. The Whitingham property owner assured everyone that it had been removed without his permission. Constable Williams said such an act could result in citations for the thief and the Church itself. Now fines and jail time entered the picture.

To make a long story short, the stone was returned to its hole, the case was quickly closed, and—at least for now—all is well.

Sadly, it isn't often I get to report on an entertaining caper like this one. But the odd thing is, the stone's original *appearance* was probably a caper, too. Whitingham history buffs have long tried to explain its sudden manifestation. The mystery of the "Materializing Monument" has never been precisely solved. Who ordered it? Who paid for it? Who put it in place? No doubt Gerald Wheeler knew the secret, but he took it with him to the grave.

If you have any interest in seeing the Brigham Young Monument, better do it soon, before it vanishes again. You can photograph words that are—at least for now—securely etched upon its chiseled surface. In its entirety, the missing and returned commemoration reads: "Brigham Young, born on this spot (in) 1801—a man of much courage and superb equipment."

৵ SECTION V. ৵
WONDERS WILL NEVER CEASE

Wherein we consider a limited potpourri of paranormal problems. Though the number of such oddities is legion, we'll limit ourselves to three. . .

❧ THE GREAT BURLINGTON UFO CRASH ❧

A little before noon on July 2, 1907, three men stood chatting on the corner of Church and College Streets in downtown Burlington.

The routine rumor of this peaceful lakeside city of 20,000 people was suddenly shattered by a terrific explosion. Windows rattled, animals howled, and bewildered pigeons flapped spastically through the air. The three men looked around in terror.

What was it? Too loud for a gunshot. A cannon, maybe? Or pranksters prematurely touching off 4th of July fireworks?

Hundreds of people dashed outside or hurried to their windows to investigate. Those first on the scene in front of the Standard Coal and Ice Company were horrified to find a horse flattened in the street. Somebody guessed it had been killed by lightning. Several men rushed to its side, only to back off again as the dazed animal struggled unsteadily to its feet.

Only stunned. But by what?

Thanks to The Burlington Free Press, and other publications of the day, testimony was collected at the scene. One individual was sure he had observed a mysterious flying object, a glowing ball, that struck the center of College Street, bounced, knocked down the horse, then soared off into the sky.

Alvaro Adsit, co-owner of Ferguson and Adsit's Store, reported a "ball of fire" descending in front of Hall's Furniture Store. When the sphere was about 15 feet above ground, Mr. Adsit said, it "exploded with a deafening sound." It had been 8 or

10 inches in diameter, he said, with a surrounding yellow-tinged halo measuring about 10 feet.

Mr. W.P. Dodds of the Equitable Life Insurance Building said the ball, "... was moving... from the northwest [over the Howard Bank Building] and gradually descending." But, he adds, "I did not see it at the moment of the explosion or afterward; no damage resulted so far as is known to me."

For a final dramatic detail, the Burlington Free Press reporter concluded by saying, "The unusual disturbance was followed in a few minutes by a downpour of rain, which continued, with brief interruption, for nearly two hours."

~ ~

For a measure of clarification, let's move back to the trio of men chatting on the corner of Church and College Streets. They were Vermont's Ex-Governor Urban Woodbury and Vermont's Roman Catholic Bishop John S. Michaud, two highly credible witnesses. Governor Woodbury said he thought an explosion had occurred; when he turned he expected to see smoke, flying bricks, and other damage.

Bishop Michaud got the best look at the airborne object. Here are his exact words: "I was standing on the corner of Church and College Streets, just in front of the Howard Bank and facing east, engaged in conversation with Ex-Governor Woodbury and Mr. A.A. Buell, when, without the slightest indication or warning we were startled by what sounded like a most unusual and terrific explosion, evidently very nearby. My first impression was that it was some explosive shot from the upper portion of the Hall Furniture Store."

In describing the object, he was very precise: "I observed a torpedo-shaped body some 300 feet away, stationary in appearance and suspended in the air about 50 feet above the tops of the buildings. ...[I]t was about six feet long by eight inches in diameter, the shell-cover having a dark appearance, with here and there tongues of fire issuing from spots on the surface resembling red-hot unburnished copper.

"Although stationary when first noticed," the Bishop

continued, "this object soon began to move, rather slowly, and disappeared over Dolan Brothers' store [on the corner of College Street and Mechanic Lane, heading] southward. As it moved, the covering seemed rupturing in places and through these the intensely red flames issued...

"When first seen, it was surrounded by a halo of dim light, some 20 feet in diameter. There was no odor that I am aware of perceptible after the disappearance of the phenomenon, nor was there any damage done so far as was known to me."

The experience must have been rather disturbing for the Bishop. He later added, "I hope I may never hear or see a similar phenomenon...."

Apparently we have two dissimilar descriptions of the same object. Or could there in fact have been two objects in the sky, one round, the other torpedo-like? Or was it a single object viewed from different perspectives?

Giving more weight to Bishop Michaud's very detailed description, we must ask what airborne object, in 1907, was surrounded by a glowing halo, could stop and start, progress slowly, cause a tremendous concussion, and give off jets of fire?

And just how did it "disappear"? Did it simply drop out of sight, or did it literally vanish? Or perhaps there is another possibility.

As you can see, we're left with a major puzzle: Exactly what did Burlingtonians see on that otherwise clear July morning? Was it some freak weather phenomenon? William H. Alexander, Burlington's weather expert at the time, guessed it was "ball lightning." But that doesn't correspond closely enough with witness testimony.

Airplanes were out of the question; back then there were fewer than five in the whole USA. Surely the object's behavior was not that of a meteor; changing speed, stopping dead, then moving on. And today's concerns ranging from sonic booms to international terrorism were still a long way in the future.

To add to the puzzle and to make this a modern mystery, an international scientific research organization called "The Center for the Study of Extraterrestrial Intelligence," has reinterpreted the Burlington event as a possible UFO landing. . . or crash.

Such a possibility was perhaps beyond the pale in 1907. Kenneth Arnold's vision of saucers flying in formation over Mt. Rainier wouldn't take place until 1947. New Mexico wasn't even a state yet, so the puzzling events of the Roswell "crash" in July exactly 40 years later would have seemed like something out of H.G. Wells's *The Shape of Things to Come*. Barney and Betty Hill and their interstellar rendezvous in the White Mountains of New Hampshire would not occur until 1961.

In short, no one in 1907 was thinking about UFOs and Flying Saucers. If the UFO assessment is correct, and the object did crash, what has happened to its remains? Were they carted off by members of the souvenir-hungry crowd? Are they embedded in the earth somewhere east of South Winooski Avenue? Or are they packed away in forgotten wooden crates in the endless bowels of the University of Vermont?

I wonder if anyone knows.

✌ VERMONT'S HIDDEN POPULATION ✍

In 1977 Sandra Mansi snapped a photo of what might be Champ, the so-called "Lake Champlain Monster." In 1979, when she released it to the press—including *The New York Times, Time magazine, The Today Show,* and hundreds of other media—the whole world quickly learned about Vermont's underwater wonder. Ms. Mansi's odyssey was dramatized on NBC TV's *Unsolved Mysteries* and Fox's *Sightings.* A 90-minute documentary was produced in Japan. Hundreds of books, magazines, and newspapers flaunted the story. Over the years, Lake Champlain's elusive critter became a cryptozoological superstar.

But what we didn't know is that an equally mysterious photograph was snapped that same year, though oddly it was never exploited by the press. Instead, it was quickly filed away, kept a secret, and mostly forgotten by all but a few believers and skeptics.

This remarkable "whatzit" was photographed on land, in the depths of the forest, once again raising the question: Are there really monsters in our midst?

This is not, of course, a new question.

For hundreds of years Vermonters have been seeing strange things in the woods. Some of these encounters have been documented. Enough sightings are on record to provide a continuing ribbon of weirdness starting, perhaps, in 1609 with Samuel de Champlain himself. He heard Native American stories of oversized, hairy men who hid in the dense woods. Monsieur Champlain disregarded the stories as fantasies.

Perhaps he was too hasty.

Historically, the first recorded encounter came in 1759 with a man named Duluth, a scout with Roger's Rangers. While they were retreating after the raid on the Abenaki settlement of Odanak, near Memphremagog Bay, the men "were ever being annoid, for naught reason, by a large black bear, who would throw large pinecones and nuts down upon us from trees and ledges, the Indians being also disgusted, and knowe him, and call him Wejuk or Wet Skine."

Wet Skin, renamed "Slipperyskin" by the European settlers, was still around as Vermont's Northeast Kingdom began to grow. There, during the late 18th and early 19th centuries, the towns of Lemington, Maidstone, Morgan, Victory, and Westmore, were routinely harassed by this fearsome oddity. Those who confronted the thing identified it as a bear of tremendous proportions. It terrorized the inhabitants with a series of hostile pranks, including tearing up their gardens, frightening their livestock, stealing food, destroying machinery, and attacking their children with stones. All attempts to trap it or kill it were predictably unsuccessful.

But here's the thing: Old Slipperyskin was like no bear anyone had ever seen. Not only was it extraordinarily intelligent, but it always walked on its hind legs, never on all fours.

Recently, researchers have taken a new look at this old tale. Could Slipperyskin have been something other than an uber-bear?

Most likely.

Whatever it may have been, it seemed to be trying to discourage the encroachment of human settlement into an area that had long been its own domain. Suspects more tangible than myth include a disgruntled Indian, a hermitical eccentric, or quite possibly what we know today as Bigfoot.

❧ PHOTOGRAPIC EVIDENCE ❧

This oversized hirsute hominid has never gone away, suggesting that if it exists outside the realm of conventional zoology, there must be a breeding pool large enough to sustain a population. He, she, or it is still sighted with alarming regularity, even in populated parts of the state. Certainly there have been as many Bigfoot sightings as Champ sightings; it's just that Champ gets all the publicity. And the existing photograph—seemingly of Bigfoot—though never widely publicized, suggests that he, like Champ, is not a hallucination.

The photo itself is almost as mysterious as the image it contains. Its primary investigator, Dr. Warren Cook of Castleton State College, is dead. He was part of the "conspiracy" that hushed up the picture's existence. During my research I was given a letter from Dr. Cook to Don Cochrane who, in 1987, was working at what today is known as the Mountain Top Inn & Resort in Chittenden.

I phoned Mr. Cochrane on July 21, 2006 hoping for clarification. It was a very brief non-conversation. When I told him what I was calling about he said, "I don't want to talk about it," and hung up the phone.

Because of this gothic reception, the mystery deepened. My most direct links to the photo were either deceased or not talking.

Nonetheless, I was determined to sort things out for a magazine article, but my deadline was becoming near-lethal. I began placing a series of panicky phone calls. A lot of people in the Chittenden area recalled something about the incident, but no one could give me specifics. Who took the photo? Where, exactly, was it taken? Why was there an apparent cloak of silence over its existence?

When I connected with Roger Hill, Activities and Facilities Director at the Mountain Top Inn & Resort, he recalled a few telling details. "What I remember about the picture," he said, "was that it was taken on forest service property, near here, which we have a permit to use for skiing and horseback riding. In the foreground the picture shows a couple of stringers running across a stream. That's the beginning of a bridge that was being built for cross-country skiing. I'm not sure if the photo was taken by Don Cochrane, but he was involved in one way or another. After it was developed it came back and somebody started looking rather oddly at that figure in the background. Some of us wonder what the heck it is."

There in the trees, as if it had been watching them all along, was what appeared to be the stocky torso and head of a gorilla. Its featureless face seemed surrounded with silvery hair.

Through another series of phone conversations, including chats with former inn owners, I was able to piece together a more complete version of the story. The photo was apparently taken by Don Cochrane in October of 1977, 2.9 miles into the Chittenden woods. He was accompanied by two other men.

No one noticed anything unusual until they examined the developed prints. Not knowing what to make of the puzzle in his picture, Mr. Cochrane brought it to the attention of Dr. Cook. For many years Dr. Cook had actively investigated the possibility that Vermont might be home to a hidden Bigfoot tribe. This photograph seemed to back that up.

Dr. Cook submitted it and the negative to a prestigious photographic lab in Los Angeles who assured him the negative had not been tampered with. In a letter to Mr. Cochrane, Dr. Cook wrote, "I think I can assert, without doubt, that whatever caused the image on your negative, it was transitory."

Dr. Cook and his team had visited the spot to try to identify anything that could have been mistaken for a giant ape. After taking more pictures, they cleared away the bushes within 60 feet of where the image had appeared. "We found no upturned stump, nor stump, or hole of any size to account for the big, black image in your photo."

In July of 2006 I asked photographer and photo analyst Sarah Vogelsang—who occasionally works with Paranormal Investigators of New England—to take a new look at the mystery photo. Because we did not possess the negative, Ms. Vogelsang was at a disadvantage. With some frustration, she told me, "I can't seem to figure it out!" Her cautious conclusion was as follows: "My analysis of the photo, given that it is the only evidence presented at this time, is not enough to convince me that the dark object in the image is a living ape-like creature (assuming that is what we are looking for) due to the lack of highlights, but it is also convincing enough to believe otherwise."

❧ MYSTERIES AND MORE MYSTERIES ❧

To me, Ms. Vogelsang's analysis of the photo is an apt metaphor for the whole Vermont Bigfoot enigma: People repeatedly see something, but they don't know what it is.

The point seems to be that it—whatever it is—has been surfacing for centuries. While the skeptics, along with most local media, dismiss Bigfoot sightings as nothing but a pile of ape droppings, the persistence of evidence suggests something mysterious is out there. Could there be a hidden population in our midst? Do families of Bigfoots live in little enclaves in the most inaccessible regions of our state? Or are they migratory, passing through Vermont according to some as yet undiscovered timetable in the manner of catamounts and salmon?

That is all part of the mystery. What we have as of this writing is dots of evidence. And it's time for investigators with uninhibited curiosity to connect those dots.

One such dot is an early encounter reported October 18, 1879 on the front page of *The New York Times*. "Pownal, VT., Oct. 17—Much excitement prevailed among the sportsmen of this vicinity over the story that a wild man was seen on Friday last by two young men while hunting in the mountains south of Williamstown. The young men describe the creature as being about five feet high, resembling a man in form and movement, but covered all over with bright red hair, and having a long straggling beard, and with very wild eyes.

"When first seen, the creature sprang from behind a rocky cliff and started for the woods near by. When mistaking it for a bear or other wild animal, one of the men fired, and, it is thought, wounded it, for with fierce cries of pain and rage, it turned on its assailants, driving them before it at high speed. They lost their guns and ammunition in their flight and dared not return for fear of encountering the strange being."

Even in those days stories of Vermont's hidden hairy hominids were well known. The article goes on, "There is an old story, told many years ago, of a strange animal frequently seen along the range of the Green Mountains resembling a man in appearance, but so wild that no one could approach it near enough to tell what it was or where it dwells. From time to time, hunting parties, in the early days of the town, used to go out in pursuit of it, but of late years no trace of it has been seen, and this story, told by young men who claim to have seen it, revives again the old story of the wildman of the mountains. There is talk of making up a party to go in search of the creature."

Note how myth and fact collide in this 19th century accounting.

But it's facts we're interested in, and the evidence continues to pile up—hundreds of examples, sometimes solitary sightings, sometimes clusters—right up until the present day.

In February 1951 lumbermen John Rowell and a Mr. Kennedy returned to their logging operation in Sudbury Swamp. They discovered a canvas-covered oil drum had vanished overnight. Somehow the 450-pound barrel had traveled from a tractor to a spot several hundred feet into the woods. Examining the ground revealed dozens of huge human-like footprints. Mr. Rowell photographed the tracks with his Polaroid. They measured 20 inches long and 8 inches wide.

In the early 1960s, William Lyford, a Plainfield farmer, heard his cows making a ruckus. Heading out to check, he saw a tall, hairy creature standing upright. When Mr. Lyford aimed his flashlight at it, the figure took off running into the darkness, leaving yet another baffled witness.

In the 1970s and '80s a series of confrontations began in Chittenden, where the mystery photo was taken. One of the most dramatic involved the pseudonymous Everett Pike. In the spring of 1984 Mr. Pike was wakened by loud screaming in his dooryard. This long-time hunter wasn't usually easy to spook, but he told investigator Ted Pratt, "I just couldn't get out of bed. It was a horrible scream. It lasted five to seven seconds." His terror escalated when he heard something rip his cellar door off its hinges. Whatever it was noisily cased the basement, then fled, leaving a handprint, a footprint, and a broken door made of solid two-inch oak.

When I spoke with James Guyette of Hartland, he recounted his especially poignant encounter of April, 1984. It was still clear in his mind. I suspect such episodes imprint themselves indelibly on the memory.

He says he was driving north on Interstate 91 at about six o'clock in the morning. When he was within sight of the Hartland Dam, Mr. Guyette spotted a "huge hairy animal-man" swinging its arms as it walked along the roadside about 100 yards away. He says it was tall and lanky, but unquestionably walking upright on two legs. The creature moved down the bank beside the interstate heading west, away from the Connecticut River. Later, when telling his wife of the reality-altering encounter, Mr. Guyette found himself weeping.

~ RECENT EVENTS ~

1759, 1879, 1951, 1960, 1984—it is easy to relegate all such sightings to the distant past. But that would be a mistake. Such events are still happening on a regular basis. We just don't know it because local newspapers rarely report them.

For example, Mr. Rowell delivered his Polaroids to the Middlebury newspaper yet they were never published. Noah Hoffenberg of the *Bennington Banner* is the great exception. He covered a cluster of local Bigfoot sightings without ever putting tongue in cheek.

One such story is the September, 2003 experience of Ray Dufresne of Winooski, Vermont. After dropping his daughter off at Southern Vermont College in Bennington, Ray headed north on Route 7, beginning the 125-mile drive back to his home.

It was about 7:00 p.m.

When he had reached the highest elevation between

Bennington and Manchester, Mr. Dufresne noticed something moving in a narrow, deserted field on his right.

"What the fuck was that?" he said in the empty car.

During a recent interview at his home, he told me, "It was a big black hairy thing, walking strangely. Long hairy arms; the body was huge. It was a lot bigger than me. I'm 220, so this must have been over 270. A lot over. Over 6 feet. Wider. Beefier. I just couldn't believe it. Must be a man in a gorilla suit, I thought."

He lost sight of it as it moved east into the woods of Glastenbury Mountain, an area where, over the years, many strange sights and sounds have been reported.

"I kept driving," Mr. Dufresne said. "There was nothing around. No cars, no houses. It was a desolate place. Now I kick myself because I didn't go back and investigate."

So what do you think you saw, I asked him.

"I'm not saying it's Bigfoot," he said. "I was never a Bigfoot believer. But I saw what I saw and I can't change what I saw."

The truth of Mr. Dufresne's tale was buttressed when other people reported similar sightings in the same area.

After Ray's story appeared in the *Bennington Banner*, San Francisco writer Doug Dorst came forth to report that he had seen a similar creature a week earlier as he was driving toward Bennington College to give a reading. He saw what Ray did not: the creature's face, which he described as light brown.

Two women—Sadelle Wiltshire and Ann Mrowicki—said they had also seen the "beast" the same night as Mr. Dufresne. They estimated they'd been as close as 10 feet away.

While all concerned admit a misidentification or hoax might be possible, Ray Dufresne says it definitely wasn't a bear. As a lifelong hunter, he can easily identify a bear. Besides, bears will not walk on their hind legs for any great distance.

A hoax is another matter, but "the man in a gorilla suit" solution is pretty far-fetched. And dangerous. Armed men in pickups routinely patrol that isolated area, many of whom would be delighted to bag Vermont's first Bigfoot. Any trickster dressed in a gorilla suit would be about as safe as a jokester wearing antlers in the woods during deer season.

❧ THE MARSHFIELD MONSTER ❧

I'll conclude with a more recent sighting investigated by Christopher Noel, a writer and teacher at Vermont College. As an investigator for the national Bigfoot Field Researchers Organization, Christopher has examined many Vermont Bigfoot experiences. "In May, 2006," he told me, "two thirteen-year-old cousins, a girl and a boy, were visiting their grandparents' cabin in Marshfield. While they were out on their ATVs traveling along a disused logging road, they were stopped by a fallen tree. As they were turning around, a figure they described as seven feet tall and hairy rose then dashed on into the forest."

Christopher says, "Seven feet always seems to be a fallback height when describing these things."

When he interviewed family members, the cousins' uncle told of another dramatic encounter in the same general area, around 1980: "He recalled that when he was 19 he and a few friends were doing some night fishing at the reservoir. Someone or something in the bushes began throwing large rocks over their heads and into the water. It was as if someone was trying to scare them. This sort of thing has happened in many cases. It is not as if the rocks are aimed to hit anyone, only frighten them. It usually works."

❧ A MATTER FOR EXPERTS ❧

There are hundreds of additional examples. One is either convinced or one isn't. Having looked at some of the evidence—anecdotes, castings, hair, even scat—we still gravitate back to the pictures. Did Sanda Mansi photograph Champ? Did the Chittenden team snap the state's first Bigfoot photo?

The latter is in no way a hoax. It has been kept out of the public eye for almost 30 years. No one had anything to gain by concealing what may be the best evidence Vermont can offer about Bigfoot's existence. We don't even know why it was hushed up. To protect the photographer from inevitable ridicule? To preserve the inn's reputation as a safe vacation getaway as opposed to a reservation for unknown animals?

Mystery wrapped in mystery.

In trying to make sense of all this, I sought out an expert, Loren Coleman, an internationally-known anthropologist and Bigfoot authority in Portland, Maine. Mr. Coleman is the author of *Bigfoot!: The True Story of Apes in America* (NY: Paraview Pocket —Simon and Schuster, 2003).

I asked him the obvious questions. For example, I said, "I think any animal living here in Vermont can occasionally be found beside the road, dead. Yet, as far as I know, no Bigfoot body has ever been found there or anywhere else. What do you make of that?"

"Why do we find roadkill?" he said. "Because those animals are not very bright. Yes, deer, moose, raccoons, and a few bear get killed on the roads, but if there are some intelligent biped hairy hominoids out there, they appear to be too smart to be killed by a run-in with a car."

"Would you care to predict the future?" I asked. "What do you think will be the final outcome? Will Bigfoot join Mountain Gorillas in the biology books? Or is it more likely to remain in the realm of folklore and cryptozoology?"

Mr. Coleman seemed to ponder the question. "I sense that a new great ape, probably discovered in Asia or Oceania, will surprise us all in the next 25 years, perhaps on the island of Sumatra. But as far as the classic American Bigfoot, I think it might be another 100 years until they are discovered. We have to be patient. It took 60 to 70 years to discover and capture the first giant panda and the Mountain Gorilla. Bigfoot will be an even bigger wonder.

"Verification for zoology and biology must come with a live capture, and DNA/blood samples—or a dead body. It's that simple. No body, no proof they exist. I understand that, but, of course, am in the 'live capture' camp, as far as proving they exist."

So the evidence gained thus far, whether anecdotal or physical, isn't enough. And the "Bigfoot photo," whether real, hoax, or misperceived shadows, keeps the mystery alive.

❧ THE END OF THE WORLD . . . VERMONT STYLE ❧

Tsunamis. Tornadoes. Avalanches. Earthquakes. Mudslides. Terrorism and war.

Religious leaders and crackpots are spouting myriad end-of-the-world scenarios. It feels like disasters are all around us.

As I write this there is a doomsday group traveling around the country with a "Bible Code" that says the world will end this year, 2011, on May 21. If you're reading this it probably didn't happen.

Others believe the world will end next year, because 2012 is the year the Mayan calendar runs out. Makes sense, right?

The point is, we could be living in the final days. The Rapture might be just around the corner. Even dyed-in-the-wool skeptics like me are beginning to get just a wee bit edgy.

But take heart. Here in the Green Mountain State predictions of gloom and doom are business as usual. Over the years many earnest Vermonters have frightened themselves and their neighbors with grim prophesies concerning the end of days.

Just for fun, here are three of my favorites.

❧ THE ROD OF DOOM ❧

1799. Middletown Springs, Vermont. A religious zealot named Nathaniel Wood Sr. got tossed out of the local Congregational church, so he decided to start his own church, dubbing his followers the "New Israelites."

"Priest Wood," as he was called by his eccentric flock, began using a Y-shaped dowsing rod during his sermons. His "magic stick" would tap and twitch in answer to questions from the congregation.

Today we might ask whether it was more likely that God or Wood was communicating through wood? But Priest Wood's followers had no doubt; they saw the tapping, gyrating rod as tangible proof of divine guidance from the Great Beyond.

Sure enough, Priest Wood's following increased. With God speaking directly and exclusively to them, Priest Wood's disciples were confident The Good Lord would lead them to endless riches (buried somewhere in the vicinity of Middletown Springs) to enable them to build their New Jerusalem.

The rod even ordered them to erect a glorious temple. Then, mid-construction, it instructed them to stop.

The credulous congregation stood aghast as the stick warned them about a horrific earthquake that would soon lay waste to the entire world. In fact, it gave them a specific date: January 14, 1801.

Well, the fatal day came and went and—you guessed it— nothing happened. There was a lot of hemming and hawing as Priest Wood and his few remaining loyalists took what was left of the funds, skulked off into the wilds of New York, and vanished.

↝ THE RELUCTANT PROPHETESS ↜

Almost half a century later, Melissa Warner, a timid farm woman from Bristol, had an odd supernatural encounter. During broad daylight she saw two black, human-shaped forms hovering above her house in the clear afternoon sky. When they saw her looking, they transformed into recognizable religious icons—God and Jesus—and tried to frighten her with ghastly predictions about the impending end of the world. They instructed her to spread the word at once so people could repent. The remaining days, they warned, were few in number. Unfortunately, the poor woman was just too shy to involve herself in such dramatic antics. She couldn't see herself bustling from door to door spreading Armageddon prophesies, so she failed to hold up her half of the bargain. And, thus far, God has neglected to hold up His.

❧ WILLIAM MILLER ❧

I suspect the local prophet who gets credit for frightening the most people was William Miller, who lived near Fair Haven. This farmer and bible scholar used references in Revelation and the book of Daniel to determine that the world would end sometime between March 21, 1843 and March 25, 1844.

At first he was unsure of his calculations. Then in 1832 God spoke directly to him, assuring him that he was right and commanding him to spread the word.

This persuasive Vermont prophet quickly became a popular speaker all over New England. To back him up, unearthly occurrences—earthquakes, holy visions, revolutions, and meteor showers—lent credence to his terrifying message.

The prediction went viral. Thousands of people converted to what was called Millerism. Eventually, the prophet announced the exact date the world would end: April 3, 1843. People from all over the country gave away their homes and belongings and climbed the highest hills to get a head start on their trip up to Paradise. Young women broke off engagements in order to die as virgins. Some people even killed their families and themselves, thinking that would put them at the head of the line at the Pearly Gates.

But—predictable of predictions—nothing happened.

The newly impoverished faithful reminded each other that the original prophesy had said *between* March 1843 and March 1844. So it could still happen. But the time span elapsed and the world remained intact.

Meanwhile, rechecking his calculations, Rev. Miller found his error. He had used the wrong calendar. The real doomsday would be October 22, 1844. This time for sure.

Unbelievable as it sounds, after two failed doomsdays, Millerites rallied once again. This time the frightened converts reached almost a million believers.

Suspense and mania escalated to biblical proportions and—

Well, I hope it won't ruin the end of the story if I tell you that nothing happened: The world didn't end.

At least not yet.

But next time for sure. . .

THE END
(of the book)

~ ABOUT THE AUTHOR ~

J oseph A. Citro (on right) is an expert in New England weirdness. In over a dozen publications—novels and nonfiction— he has guided readers through a dark, disturbing, and often sinister landscape traditionally portrayed with sunny skies above quaint villages. His nonfiction books include *Passing Strange, Cursed in New England*, and many more. Additionally, Mr. Citro has authored five acclaimed novels, among them *Shadow Child, Lake Monsters, Deus-X: The Reality Conspiracy* and a collection of short fiction called *Not Yet Dead*. You can reach him on Facebook or via the electronic Ouija board at . . .
BLOG: http://josephacitro.blogspot.com
WEB: http://www.josephacitro.com

Curious about other Crossroad Press books?
Stop by our site:
http://store.crossroadpress.com
We offer quality writing
in digital, audio, and print formats.

Enter the code FIRSTBOOK
to get 20% off your first order from our store!
Stop by today!

CPSIA information can be obtained at www.ICGtesting.com
Printed in the USA
LVOW121505010513

331844LV00015B/662/P